Matt pulled back, breaking the kiss before he lost what little control he had left.

"Why did you do that?" he asked in a low voice, sounding more gruff than he'd intended.

"It was your idea," Calley said softly, her fingers rubbing her cheek.

He could see redness there and knew his beard stubble had made the mark. "Damn it, Calley. All I had in mind was talking."

She tilted her head as she looked at him, confusion clouding her blue eyes. "Was it so awful?"

Awful? Was she serious? "No. It was just... unexpected." He wondered how he could explain it to her when even he didn't understand the riot of emotions churning through him.

"I'm sorry if I offended you," she said, not looking the least bit sorry to him. "I thought I was helping put your new plan into action."

"Can you at least give me a little warning next time?"

"Don't worry, Matt," she said calmly, turning toward the chuck wagon. "There won't be a next time."

He watched her disappear inside the wagon, then heard the loud clank of pots and pans, followed by a muffled oath. Matt smiled. He might have been wrong, but so was she. There would definitely be a next time.

Dear Reader,

I'm a big fan of country music and was inspired to write this story by listening to Trisha Yearwood's song "I Want To Live Again." The toe-tapping music and heartfelt lyrics are perfect for my heroine, Calley Graham, who is determined to live life to the fullest. Matt Radcliffe is a sexy cowboy who prefers to live life alone. But Calley is *hot on his trail,* which means Matt doesn't stand a chance!

I hope you enjoy Matt and Calley's story. Happy reading!

Karen Hughes

TRUEBLOOD, TEXAS

Karen Hughes

Hot on His Trail

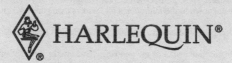

HARLEQUIN®

TORONTO • NEW YORK • LONDON
AMSTERDAM • PARIS • SYDNEY • HAMBURG
STOCKHOLM • ATHENS • TOKYO • MILAN • MADRID
PRAGUE • WARSAW • BUDAPEST • AUCKLAND

Special thanks and acknowledgment to Kristin Eckhardt
for her contribution to the TRUEBLOOD, TEXAS series

For my wonderful mother, Charol Pleiss
Special thanks to Dr. Lisa Bladt for her medical expertise

HARLEQUIN BOOKS
225 Duncan Mill Road, Don Mills,
Ontario, Canada M3B 3K9

ISBN 0-373-65084-1

HOT ON HIS TRAIL

TRUEBLOOD TEXAS

THE TRUEBLOOD LEGACY

THE YEAR WAS 1918, and the Great War in Europe still raged, but Esau Porter was heading home to Texas.

The young sergeant arrived at his parents' ranch northwest of San Antonio on a Sunday night, only the celebration didn't go off as planned. Most of the townsfolk of Carmelita had come out to welcome Esau home, but when they saw the sorry condition of the boy, they gave their respects quickly and left.

The fever got so bad so fast that Mrs. Porter hardly knew what to do. By Monday night, before the doctor from San Antonio made it into town, Esau was dead.

The Porter family grieved. How could their son have survived the German peril, only to burn up and die in his own bed? It wasn't much of a surprise when Mrs. Porter took to her bed on Wednesday. But it was a hell of a shock when half the residents of Carmelita came down with the horrible illness. House after house was hit by death, and all the townspeople could do was pray for salvation.

None came. By the end of the year, over one hundred souls had perished. The influenza virus took those in the prime of life, leaving behind an unprecedented number of orphans. And the virus knew no boundaries. By the time the threat had passed, more than thirty-seven million people had succumbed worldwide.

But in one house, there was still hope.

Isabella Trueblood had come to Carmelita in the late 1800s with her father, blacksmith Saul Trueblood, and her mother, Teresa Collier Trueblood. The family had traveled from Indiana, leaving their Quaker roots behind.

Young Isabella grew up to be an intelligent woman who had a gift for healing and storytelling. Her dreams centered on the boy next door, Foster Carter, the son of Chester and Grace.

Just before the bad times came in 1918, Foster asked Isabella to be his wife, and the future of the Carter spread was secured. It was a happy union, and the future looked bright for the young couple.

Two years later, not one of their relatives was alive. How the young couple had survived was a miracle. And during the epidemic, Isabella and Foster had taken in more than twenty-two orphaned children from all over the county. They fed them, clothed them, taught them as if they were blood kin.

Then Isabella became pregnant, but there were complications. Love for her handsome son, Josiah, born in 1920, wasn't enough to stop her from growing weaker by the day. Knowing she couldn't leave her husband to tend to all the children if she died, she set out to find families for each one of her orphaned charges.

And so the Trueblood Foundation was born. Named in memory of Isabella's parents, it would become famous all over Texas. Some of the orphaned children went to strangers, but many were reunited with their families. After reading notices in newspapers and church bulletins, aunts, uncles, cousins and grandparents rushed to Carmelita to find the young ones they'd given up for dead.

Toward the end of Isabella's life, she'd brought together more than thirty families, and not just her orphans. Many others, old and young, made their way to her doorstep, and Isabella turned no one away.

At her death, the town's name was changed to Trueblood, in her honor. For years to come, her simple grave was adorned with flowers on the anniversary of her death, grateful tokens of appreciation from the families she had brought together.

Isabella's son, Josiah, grew into a fine rancher and married Rebecca Montgomery in 1938. They had a daughter, Elizabeth Trueblood Carter, in 1940. Elizabeth married her neighbor William Garrett in 1965, and gave birth to twins Lily and Dylan in 1971, and daughter Ashley a few years later. Home was the Double G ranch, about ten miles from Trueblood proper, and the Garrett children grew up listening to stories of their famous great-grandmother, Isabella. Because they were Truebloods, they knew that they, too, had a sacred duty to carry on the tradition passed down to them: finding lost souls and reuniting loved ones.

PROLOGUE

Texas Children's Hospital
Houston, Texas, 1992

DR. PAULA BENNING, one of Houston's busiest pediatric cardiologists, stood outside the door of the consultation room, her stomach twisting in dread. She loved every part of her profession—except this one.

A headache throbbed in her left temple, a signal that her blood sugar was low. She knew she should eat something before she broke the news, or at least find a carton of orange juice. But she'd learned early on in her career that delaying unpleasant tasks only made them harder. So she took a deep breath as she reached for the doorknob, then walked inside.

A man and a woman sat on the worn plaid sofa, their faces drawn and their hands clenched together. They looked up at her, guarded hope reflected in their eyes. Dr. Benning glanced hastily at her watch. A signal that she didn't have time to waste. *Get in and get out.* In her thirteen years of practice, she'd learned that was the best way to deliver devastating news. Best for her, anyway.

Walt Graham rose to his feet, pulling his wife along with him. "Is Calley all right?"

"She's in stable condition now," Dr. Benning confirmed.

"I've never been so scared," Liv Graham confessed, her voice cracking. A petite woman, she looked almost as frail as her daughter. They both had the same wide-set blue eyes and flaxen blond hair. "Calley couldn't catch her breath and she was so pale. I didn't know what to do."

She glanced up at her husband, a detective with the Houston police force. Walt Graham wore his worry in the deep lines etched in his forehead and between his thick, dark brows.

Dr. Benning wished she didn't know so much about the Grahams. Wished she didn't know that they'd struggled with infertility for years before they'd finally been blessed with a daughter. Liv Graham, a renowned local photographer, had been past forty when she'd conceived Calley, automatically classifying the pregnancy as high-risk. But she'd delivered a healthy baby girl, then went on to chronicle the first fifteen years of her daughter's life with incredible black-and-white photographs that had brought Liv recognition throughout the state.

Ironically, one of those photographs of Calley, her golden pigtails flying as she leaped toward the sky, graced a wall in the ICU, where the girl now lay cocooned in a hospital bed, tethered to earth by an IV line and a heart monitor.

Dr. Benning cleared her throat. She'd put off the inevitable long enough. "Perhaps you should sit down."

Walt Graham ignored her suggestion, his green eyes intent on her face. He stepped forward and curled one large hand around the top of a chair, his knuckles bleached white. "What's wrong?"

Liv Graham forced a smile, looking back and forth

between the two of them. "Nothing's wrong, Walt. Calley is fine. Right, Dr. Benning?"

"I'm afraid the preliminary tests tell us otherwise."

The blood drained from Liv's face. "What do you mean?"

Dr. Benning motioned them toward the sofa. "Please, sit down."

They obeyed without protest, walking numbly to the sofa. Dr. Benning had seen that same stoic reaction numerous times before. It was the mind's defense mechanism for dealing with shock. A mechanism that would fade soon enough. She only hoped she'd be gone before it did. Her headache had spread to the other temple and now threatened to turn into one of her rare migraines.

She pulled a chair close to the sofa and sat down, folding her hands together in her lap. "Calley has a condition called myocarditis."

Liv Graham shook her head. "I don't understand."

"Myocarditis is an inflammation of the heart muscle," Dr. Benning explained. "It can be caused by a variety of conditions. However, in Calley's case, we believe it was brought on by a viral infection."

"An infection?" Walt frowned. "But she hasn't been sick."

Liv clasped his arm. "Last month, remember? She had the sniffles. But the pediatrician told us it was hay fever. He put her on antihistamines. Is that why this happened? Should he have given her something else instead?"

Dr. Benning shook her head. "There's really no way to pinpoint how this occurred. But there was nothing that either you or Calley could have done to prevent it."

Denial darkened Liz Graham's blue eyes. "There must be some mistake. Calley's always been so healthy. She's had all her immunizations and never missed her yearly checkup."

"I'm afraid there's no mistake," Dr. Benning said softly.

Walt's jaw tightened. "How long will she be sick?"

Dr. Benning hesitated. "Myocarditis weakens the heart muscle. Some patients recover while others…." She shook her head. "It's simply too soon to give you a prognosis."

"Can't you do something?" Liv asked, looking confused. "Surgery or medication? Surely something can be done to reverse it."

"She's receiving ACE inhibitors to improve her heart function, and diuretics to decrease the fluid retention. At this point, we plan to monitor her condition and see if we can get it under control."

"And if you can't?" Walt asked.

"Then we'll have to look at all the available options and select the best one for Calley."

Liv shook her head. "That's not good enough. I need to know what's going to happen to my little girl. She's only fifteen!"

"In the worst case scenario," Dr. Benning said gently, "Calley would need a heart transplant."

Liv Graham gasped and reached for her husband's hand. Walt sat silently beside her. At last he looked up and asked in a strained voice, "Are you telling us she could die?"

"We're certainly not at that point yet," Dr. Benning assured them. She could see the anger and pain now swirling in Liv Graham's eyes. The numbness was beginning to fade.

Dr. Benning stood up, more than ready to give the Grahams some privacy. "I've ordered some more tests. We'll talk again after the results are in."

"Thank you, Dr. Benning," Walt said stiffly. His wife sat mutely beside him.

Dr. Benning nodded, then walked toward the door. As it closed behind her she could hear the first anguished sobs of Calley's mother.

"I won't let her go," Liv cried. "I'll never, ever let her go."

CHAPTER ONE

Ten years later

CALLEY GRAHAM paced across the second floor of the Double G ranch house, ignoring the chirp of the cell phone in her purse. She'd arrived early for her job interview at Finders Keepers—two hours early, as a matter of fact. Patience had never been one of her virtues.

It had been three days since she'd seen their advertisement for a temporary private investigator in the classifieds section of the *San Antonio Express-News*. And it had only taken her about five seconds to decide this was her opportunity to escape. After a little planning, she'd made a furtive call for an interview.

Her first step toward freedom.

Calley had packed her suitcase this morning, leaving San Antonio before sunrise to avoid detection. Then she'd waited at a coffee shop until it was time to make the short drive to Trueblood, Texas. The housekeeper had let her in the front door and directed her to the offices located on the second floor of the sprawling ranch house.

Finders Keepers was run by Dylan Garrett and his twin sister, Lily Garrett Bishop. With a little research, she'd learned that the ranch had apparently been in the Garrett family for generations. After careers in law enforcement, both Dylan and Lily had returned home to start an agency that specialized in finding missing persons.

Calley closed her eyes, mentally reviewing her job pitch. Unfortunately, graduating from a home study course on private investigation didn't sound very impressive. So she'd padded her résumé with a degree in criminal justice and listed several cases of freelance investigative work. Thankfully, the confidential nature of this business made it impossible for the Garretts to verify her work experience. She wanted this job too much to ruin her chances by telling the truth.

The sound of a plaintive whine made her open her eyes. At her feet sat a full-grown Irish setter, its big brown eyes gazing dolefully up at her. He raised one paw and placed it on her knee.

She laughed and knelt down, stroking the dog's silky head. "Hello, sweetheart," she murmured. "What's your name?"

The setter scooted closer to her, his eyelids drooping as Calley scratched behind his ears.

"I used to have a dog just like you," she said, a lump forming in the back of her throat as she thought of Trixie, her cuddly cocker spaniel. Trixie had been gone when Calley had returned from the hospital ten years ago. Her mother had sold Calley's pet, fearing it might carry too many germs. She took a deep breath and swallowed hard, refusing to let the pain of the past overwhelm her. She needed to concentrate on her future. With a little luck, it would start today.

"His name is Shiloh," a voice said behind her.

She stood and turned to see a young woman with chin-length auburn hair and sparkling green eyes.

Calley stroked Shiloh's head. "He's a wonderful dog."

"And ornery," the woman said, moving behind the wide oak desk. "He steals the pens off my desk and buries them in the south pasture." She reached into a drawer and pulled out a box that made Shiloh trot up to her, his tail wagging furiously behind him.

The woman dropped a dog biscuit into his mouth, then shooed him onto a braided rug near the bookcases along the wall. Brushing her hands together, she turned back to Calley. "I'm Carolyn Mulholland, the office assistant for Finders Keepers. Are you here about a case?"

"Actually, I'm here to interview for the job. My name is Calley Graham."

Carolyn's eyes widened. "Oh, I'm sorry. You're early. And I guess I didn't expect you to be so young."

"I'm twenty-five," Calley said, then wished she'd bitten her tongue instead. What if the Garretts held her age against her? Maybe she should have added a couple more years to her already fictitious résumé.

"May I get you a cup of coffee or a soda while you wait?" Carolyn motioned toward the minikitchen area behind her desk. "It may be a while yet."

"No, I'm fine," Calley assured her. Then her purse began to chirp again.

Carolyn furrowed her brow. "Is that your phone?"

"Yes." Calley reached reluctantly inside her purse and pulled out the small cellular.

"I'll give you some privacy," Carolyn said, misreading Calley's reticence and walking into one of the inner offices.

With a resigned sigh, Calley opened the flip phone,

hesitated a moment, then switched it off. She couldn't deal with her mother right now. And she definitely couldn't tell her about the impending job interview. Not when Liv Graham routinely sabotaged Calley's bids for independence. All for her own good. Or at least, that's how her mother saw it.

It had started when she'd taken Calley out of high school after the heart condition had been diagnosed, claiming it would be easier and safer to home-school her. Then she'd scared away all of Calley's friends, warning them that if they inadvertently infected Calley with a cold or the flu, they could kill her.

But it was her mother's fear that was contagious. It had torn her parents' marriage apart. Her father was now remarried and living in Florida, leaving Calley alone to deal with her mother's obsessive love. Liv Graham had been so afraid that her daughter would die that she hadn't let her live.

Now that was all about to change.

If she could get this job. Calley walked over to the polished wooden rail bordering the second floor, wishing she knew what would impress the Garretts. What would make them believe she was the perfect candidate for the job? She looked out over the great room below, noting the massive stone fireplace and the heavy, exposed beams. It looked as if the house had once been smaller, then expanded to accommodate a growing family.

Was that the answer to her question? Family ties? It made sense, considering Dylan and Lily Garrett had chosen to open a business together and run it out of their old family home. Especially when you considered the focus of the agency—to reunite people with their loved ones.

Family ties. That was the key. Something she could use to her advantage.

Even if she believed some family ties had to be broken.

"WE HAVE TO find Matt Radcliffe." Lily Garrett Bishop sat propped up in bed, several eiderdown pillows supporting her. "He's the last beneficiary in Violet Mitchum's will." She watched her brother pace across her bedroom floor. He hadn't even heard her. Not surprising, considering he'd been strangely preoccupied since Christmas.

"Dylan?"

He stopped and looked up at her. "What's the matter? Is it the baby?"

She placed one hand protectively over her swollen belly. Only six months pregnant, she'd gone into premature labor a week ago. Fortunately, the doctors had been able to stop it.

Her husband, Cole, had been at his ranch, overseeing its sale to his ranch foreman, Manny Peres. He'd rushed home, the ink still wet on the bill of sale.

Both he and Dylan hovered over her, along with her father. Treating her like a fragile porcelain doll. She'd meekly accepted their coddling at first, terrified that she might lose her baby. But she was feeling much stronger now, and though she had every intention of following the doctor's orders by staying in bed, that didn't mean she couldn't still play an active role in Finders Keepers.

If only her overprotective brother would let her.

"Sit down, Dylan," she ordered. "You're making me dizzy."

He immediately complied, his brow creased with

worry. "Are you sure you're all right? Do you want me to call your doctor? Or Cole? He's at the construction site, going over those changes in your house plans with the builder."

"I'm fine," she assured him. "And so is your niece or nephew."

Dylan reached out one hand and placed it on her distended belly. A small smile tipped up the corner of his mouth. "He's kicking up a storm in there."

"Tell me about it," she said, shifting a little to assuage the slight ache in her lower back. "Although I don't understand why you're so convinced it's a boy."

"Because with a kick like that, he'll make first string placekicker on the Texas A&M football team and give his uncle Dylan free season tickets."

She laughed. "You've never heard of a girl making a college team as a kicker?"

"Sure I have," he said, leaning back in his chair. "But I'd be so busy keeping all those besotted football players away from my beautiful niece that I couldn't enjoy the game."

Lily smiled as tears pricked her eyes. It felt so good to talk about her baby's future. To believe that she'd safely carry this precious child for the next three months. She reached down and squeezed her brother's hand, silently thanking him for his loving support.

A light knock on the door made them both look up. Carolyn stuck her head inside and waved at Lily, then she turned to Dylan. "Sorry to interrupt, but there is a Calley Graham here for an interview."

Lily's brow furrowed. "Interview? What interview?"

"Oops," Carolyn muttered, as Lily struggled to sit up in bed.

"Oh, hell," Dylan muttered. "I completely forgot about her." He turned to Carolyn. "Thanks. Tell Miss Graham I'll be there in a few minutes."

Lily waited until Carolyn shut the door before she turned to her brother. "Okay, Dylan, spill it. What are you up to now?"

He set his jaw. "I'm hiring a temporary investigator for Finders Keepers."

Lily arched a brow, willing herself not to lose her temper. "When were you planning to tell me?"

"I thought you had enough to worry about."

"Please don't shut me out, Dylan. If I have to lie here and do nothing for the next three months, I'll go completely stir-crazy."

"Well, you can't go out on assignment, and we have to find Matt Radcliffe."

"I think I just said that," Lily observed ruefully. Matt Radcliffe was a beneficiary in the late Violet Mitchum's will. Widow of wealthy horse rancher and oilman Charles Mitchum, Violet had lived in a Victorian monstrosity in Pinto, Texas, until her death. Finders Keepers had been retained to find the three outstanding beneficiaries among the eight people named in Violet's will. They'd successfully located Sara Pierce and Jillian Salvini, but Matt Radcliffe had proven more elusive.

Dylan sat on the edge of her bed. "Actually, we do have a lead. Our little gift to his mother finally paid off."

Lily sat further up in bed, her interest piqued. "Where is he?"

"Somewhere in New Mexico," Dylan replied.

"That sounds a little vague."

"Exactly. That's why we need someone to go out in the field and track him down. I can't do it because of—"

"Julie," Lily finished for him. The wife of Dylan's best friend, Sebastian Cooper, had disappeared after a car-jacking over a year ago. Her brother's concern for the missing Julie Cooper had almost turned into an obsession, although lately he didn't seem as tense about her disappearance as he had been for the last few months. Had he gotten a lead on her? Or just finally given up hope of ever finding her?

Dylan gave a short nod. "I also want to stay close to home in case you need me."

Lily leaned back against the pillows, feeling useless. But maybe there was something she could do. "Let me interview Calley Graham."

"That's not necessary. I've already hired someone for the job."

She blinked. "Then why is this Graham woman here for an interview?"

He raked one hand through his brown hair. "Because I forgot to tell Carolyn to cancel the interview."

Lily wasn't surprised, given how distracted her brother had been recently. Which was further proof that he needed Lily's help. "It's really not fair to send Calley Graham away now. The least you can do is interview her, or let me do it."

"Why? I've already as much as promised the job to a man named Simms. I still need to conduct a face-to-face interview with him, but that's just a formality. He's a retired cop with a résumé a mile long."

"We could send them both out into the field," Lily suggested. "Double our chances of finding Matt Radcliffe."

Dylan stood up. "That means we'll have to pay twice as much, too."

She smiled as another idea occurred to her. "Not if we make it a contest. The first one to find Matt Radcliffe and bring him back to Texas wins the job. We'd pay expenses, of course, but no salary until the winner is hired."

Dylan stared at her for a long moment, then grinned. "I see pregnancy hasn't affected your brain cells. You're still as devious as ever."

She laughed. "I believe the word you're looking for is *creative*."

"So what happens if this Graham woman and Simms both decline our not-so-generous offer?"

She arched a brow. "Would you?"

"Not a chance. I never back down from a challenge."

"Neither would I," Lily affirmed. "We want someone with guts and tenacity to work for Finders Keepers. Someone who won't give up when he, or she, runs out of leads." She settled back against the pillows with a satisfied sigh. "The more I think about this idea, the more I like it."

"Me, too," Dylan agreed. "Once we find Radcliffe, I can finally make arrangements for Violet's memorial service."

"Then let's stop wasting time," Lily replied. "Send Calley Graham in here. Let's find out how much she really wants this job."

DYLAN SENT Calley Graham to Lily's room, then shut himself in his office. Now that the matter of finding

Radcliffe was being handled, he could concentrate on gathering evidence against his best friend.

His gaze drifted to one of the framed photographs on his wall. Taken when they were all in college, it showed him and Sebastian Cooper laughing together, their arms draped around Julie, who stood between them. Despite their lengthy friendship, Julie had always stood between them. Dylan had fallen in love with her when he was a junior at Texas A&M, but it was Sebastian she'd chosen to marry.

He'd truly wanted Sebastian and Julie to be happy together. Had grieved with Sebastian when Julie had gone missing after an apparent car-jacking last year.

And had been stunned when he'd finally discovered the truth.

Julie had run away, in fear for her life and that of her unborn child. Dylan had finally tracked her down in the tiny town of Cactus Creek, Texas. She'd given birth to a son in September. A boy she'd named Thomas. But that wasn't the biggest surprise. She'd told Dylan that Sebastian had ties to the mob. All she lacked was the evidence to prove it.

So Dylan had vowed to find the evidence, even though some part of him still didn't want to believe that Sebastian could be capable of that kind of duplicity. But there was only one way to find out.

He flipped through the Rolodex on his desk, searching for the number of Zach Logan, who had been his chief in the Dallas Police Department. If anyone would be keeping tabs on the local organized crime ring, it would be Zach. Especially since he'd been instrumental in sending its leader, J. B. Crowe, to prison last spring.

Dylan picked up the telephone.

CALLEY WAS SURPRISED to find herself directed to Lily Bishop's spacious bedroom rather than Dylan Garrett's office. She had prepared herself to face a man for this job interview, not the thoughtful, intuitive young woman who studied her now.

Lily's jet-black hair contrasted sharply against the snow-white pillow cases. Despite the fact that she was confined to bed, Lily looked nothing like an invalid. She flipped quickly through the pages of Calley's résumé, her mouth pursed in concentration.

"Your résumé is a little thin," Lily said at last.

"What I lack in experience, I make up for in creativity," Calley replied. She'd planned to sugarcoat her answers to Dylan Garrett, but she instinctively knew such a strategy wouldn't work with his sister.

Lily laid the résumé on her lap. "That's good to hear, because at the moment we're working on a tough case. Sit down and I'll tell you about it."

Calley gratefully took a chair next to the bed, her knees feeling a little shaky. She wanted this job so badly. Needed it, if she was ever to venture out on her own.

"The man we're searching for is Matthew Radcliffe. He's a beneficiary in Violet Mitchum's will. Along with a monetary gift, he's to receive one of Violet's rings and a sealed letter from her." Lily handed Calley an old photo. "He was twelve when this picture was taken. That's also the age he was the last time Violet saw him."

Calley studied the photo of a tall, lanky boy riding bareback on a dappled horse. His cowboy hat shaded his face, but she could see the proud set of his thin shoulders and the confident way he held the reins.

"Matt's mother was the Mitchums' housekeeper,"

Lily continued. "He was born and raised on the Mitchum ranch. At least until the fire."

"Fire?" Calley asked, her gaze still on the photo. She wished she could see his face.

"The Mitchums lived in a Victorian house just outside of Pinto that Charles Mitchum built for his wife in the fifties. There was a fire twenty years ago that destroyed a large part of the structure. It was after this fire that Matt and his mother, Rita, disappeared."

"What about his father?" Calley asked.

"Todd Radcliffe ran out on his family when Matt was eight years old."

Calley looked up from the photo. "I assume you've already contacted Matt's mother?"

Lily nodded. "Apparently, she and her son are not close. When we first spoke with Rita in November she had no idea where to find Matt. Although she did tell us that he calls her on Christmas."

Calley glanced up. "That was two weeks ago."

Lily smiled. "We gave Rita a small gift for her cooperation. A new cordless phone with—"

"Caller ID," Calley concluded, feeling the first tingles of excitement.

"That's right. My brother just told me she contacted Finders Keepers a few days ago." Lily reached into a thin file folder and pulled out a sheet of paper. "This is the telephone number Rita wrote down after her son called."

Calley looked at the area code. "505. That's New Mexico, isn't it?"

"Yes. Dylan traced the phone number to a roadstop café outside of White Rock, New Mexico. It's a small town just north of Santa Fe. He contacted the owner of the café. Apparently, no one there knows Matt Radcliffe.''

''Which means we can assume he was just passing through.''

Lily nodded. ''That's all we have to go on. We don't even have a description, since Rita hasn't seen her son in years.''

Calley looked at the old photo once again. ''He'll be tall and have dark hair.''

''Rita did tell us that her son has dark brown eyes,'' Lily added, handing the file to Calley. ''And that he loves horses.''

As Calley glanced at the manila file folder in her hand, then at Lily, her heart began beating double time. ''Does this mean I have the job?''

''Well, you might want to hear the conditions first.''

Calley placed the photo of Matt Radcliffe inside the folder, hoping Lily couldn't see the way her hand was shaking. She didn't give a fig about any conditions. She'd walk all the way to New Mexico if necessary.

''You won't be the only one looking for Radcliffe,'' Lily continued. ''There is another man interested in this position. He'll be on the case, too. Whoever is the first one to bring Radcliffe back here wins the job.''

Calley stood up. ''Then I'd better get started.''

Lily looked up at her. ''So you're still interested?''

''Definitely,'' Calley said, her blood racing at the thrill of competition. It had been too long since she'd felt that thrill. Much too long.

''Oh, one more thing,'' Lily added, as Calley headed for the door.

She turned. "Yes?"

"You left a blank space on your application." Lily held it up. "Do you have anyone we can contact, such as a family member, in case of an emergency?"

"No," Calley said, wishing the lie wasn't necessary. "I don't have anyone."

CHAPTER TWO

MATT RADCLIFFE stood at the corral as the sun set on the horizon, the last golden rays caressing the sparse grass and sagebrush growing along the fence. He propped one boot up on a metal rail and watched the herd of one hundred longhorn steers paw up a cloud of fine dust inside the large enclosure.

He tried to ignore the spark of excitement in his belly. But it smoldered there, refusing to be doused by good common sense. At sunup, he would embark on a fool's errand, dreamed up by Rufus Tupper, New Mexico's richest resident fool. A gentleman rancher, Rufus had never raised so much as a blister. He left that to the real cowboys, like Matt. Men who loved the land but couldn't afford to buy a ranch of their own.

That was all about to change.

"Hey, cowboy."

Matt turned to see Marla Mackovic walking up to the corral. She was a former Las Vegas showgirl who had hoped to cash in on Tupper's wealth when he'd asked her to come live at the ranch. Instead, she spent most of her time dusting his horse trophies and preparing his hangover tonics.

"I missed you at supper," she said, ambling over to him, her hands behind her back. Her overpermed hair hung like a black cloud down her back. He'd always liked Marla, even if she did wear too much makeup and perfume. But he didn't like the calculating gleam he saw in her eyes this evening.

"I had a few last-minute preparations to make."

"I brought you a piece of cherry pie." She took a step forward and placed the napkin-wrapped pastry into his hand. Warm, red filling oozed out and ran over his thumb.

"Thank you," he said, sucking the sweet filling off his knuckle. Not wanting to disappoint her, he ate the pie in three bites, though it tasted like sawdust in his mouth. He had too much at stake today to care about food.

"Rufus wants to see you before you go," she told him, her long yellow broom skirt swaying softly in the warm breeze.

"Then he'd better get his butt out here," Matt said, licking the last crumbs off his fingertips.

"He wants you to come inside. Rufus is in one of his moods. I made him a bloody Mary a little while ago and he threw it against the wall. Said the tomato juice had too much pulp in it."

Matt stared at her for a long moment. "Why do you stay here, Marla? You can do better than this."

She arched one waxed eyebrow. "Why do you?"

His jaw tightened. "I'm leaving tomorrow. And I'm not coming back."

"Take me with you," she cried, reaching out to grasp his forearm. "I can cook for you and the cowhands. Wash your clothes. Sing and dance. Anything you want."

Matt smiled. "You wouldn't like it out on the trail, Marla. There aren't any televisions or stereos or refrigerators. No indoor plumbing." He reached for the hand still clutching his arm, and gently patted her thin fingers. ''And no beauty salons to keep up this pretty manicure, either.''

She pulled her hand out of his grasp, curling it into a fist to hide the long, polished red nails. ''I don't need manicures, Matt. Or any of those other things. I just need…you.''

He swallowed a sigh. Marla didn't need him and she sure didn't love him. She just wanted someone to take care of her. She'd been looking for that someone ever since she'd run away from home at seventeen. Young and pretty and temperamental, she'd wasted the last two years of her life to be at Tupper's beck and call. Obviously, she'd finally realized that she'd never find her way into the eccentric rancher's heart.

''I'm too old for you, Marla,'' he said gently.

''You're not as old as Rufus. He's almost fifty.'' She tossed her long black curls over her shoulder. ''And you're only thirty-two.''

''And you're barely twenty. You should be out having fun. Not traipsing around on a dusty trail with a bunch of cowboys.''

''Anything is better than here,'' she muttered, then sidled closer to him, placing her small hands on his chest. ''Besides, I like you, Matt. I've always liked you.'' Her soulful brown eyes gazed up at him. ''You're so big and strong.''

Her hands slid up around his shoulders and smoothed over the biceps outlined by his chambray shirt. He inhaled the stale aroma of her heavy perfume and saw the mascara smudges beneath her eyes.

''And so brave,'' Marla whispered seductively. ''None of the other cowboys stand up to Rufus like you do.''

Her soft, voluptuous curves pressed against him, and for one brief moment Matt considered her request. It had been much too long since he'd held a woman in his arms. Maybe she could assuage the loneliness that seemed to seep into his bones during the long nights on the range.

His silence encouraged her to snake her arms around his neck and press her face into the crook of his shoulder.

"Please take me with you," she entreated in the singsong voice of a little girl. "Please, Matt."

He gently disengaged himself from her, then took a step back. "Sorry, Marla. I always travel solo."

She shrugged, a petulant pout on her lips. "Fine. Then I'll ask Boyd to take me with him."

Matt bit back a smile at the thought of Tupper's hapless nephew. "Where is Boyd going?"

"With you on the cattle drive," she retorted. "I heard Tupper tell Boyd it would make a man out of him."

"Hell," Matt muttered under his breath. This drive was going to be complicated enough without dragging along a spoiled city boy. "Don't waste your time sweet-talking Boyd, Marla. I'm the boss out on the trail and I'm not allowing any distractions on this trip. It's too important."

"Fine." Anger flared in her brown eyes. "I hope all the cattle stampede and fall off a cliff! I hope your precious horse kicks you in the head! I hope you get lost in the desert and your *cojones* dry up and fall off."

"Gracious as always, I see," he said, smiling as he reached into his pocket for the keys to his pickup truck. He tossed them to her. "You can still leave,

Marla. Anytime you want. My truck has seen a lot of miles, but it's dependable. It will take you anywhere you want to go.''

"I just want *you* to go to hell," she cried, throwing the keys back at his feet. Then she spun around and ran toward the barn.

Matt stared at the keys for a moment, then turned and walked away. Marla might change her mind when her temper cooled off. Or she might decide to mow Rufus down. Either way, he wanted to help her out. She was a sweet kid when she wasn't contemplating destruction of certain portions of his anatomy.

With Marla's curse still ringing in his ears, Matt walked to the ranch house. Heat lightning flashed across the sky.

"Where the hell have you been?"

Matt looked up to see Rufus Tupper standing on the front porch. He wore a paisley silk robe and a pair of ostrich skin cowboy boots.

"You wanted to see me?"

"Hell, yes," Rufus grumbled. "You can't leave without a proper send-off. And I'm sure as hell not gettin' out of bed before sunrise. Meet me in my study." He turned around without another word and ambled back into the house.

By the time Matt reached Rufus's study, the rancher had poured two whiskeys.

"A toast," Rufus said, handing one of the tumblers to Matt. Then he raised his own glass in the air. "To the best trail boss west of the Mississippi."

Matt took a sip of the whiskey. It burned its way into his stomach and made him feel slightly queasy. But then, so did Rufus Tupper.

Matt set down his glass. "What do you want?"

"Hell, Radcliffe," Rufus said, pouring himself another whiskey. "You always this suspicious?"

"It comes with the job. I've got to be on the lookout for rattlesnakes, coyotes and other predators."

"I'll take that as a compliment." Rufus settled into his chair. "I just want to make sure that everything is all set. I've got a lot of money riding on this bet with Lester Hobbs. In fact, we've decided to up the ante."

Matt felt himself tense. Rufus and Lester were rich men with too much time and money on their hands. One whiskey-soaked night they'd reminisced about the good old days when a man could prove his mettle by driving cattle to market. Nowadays, most cattle were transported via semitrailer truck. Cattle drives were either short jaunts from one pasture to the next, or part of a tourist package for bored city slickers who wanted to play cowboy for a week.

Rufus and Lester decided to take a trip down memory lane by recreating an old-fashioned cattle drive on the Goodnight-Loving Trail, which had run west from Central Texas to Fort Sumner, New Mexico, well over a hundred years ago. Tupper had just laughed when Matt pointed out that the drive they had routed was headed in the wrong direction, running east instead of west.

"Up the ante?" Matt echoed. "You mean you've decided to make my job even harder?"

Rufus chuckled. "Hey, if you want to win that half a million dollars, you've gotta earn it. Or have you changed your mind?"

Matt folded his arms across his chest. "Are you going to tell me the new terms of the bet or are you just going to keep wasting my time?"

Rufus swirled the whiskey in his glass. "Basically the same as before. Lester and I each send one hundred longhorn steers on a cattle drive from here to my ranch near Jacksboro, Texas. First one to pass over the property line at the Lazy R wins the race."

"And?" Matt prompted.

"And we've set the death loss at five percent. Which means if more than five steers die on the trail, the bet is forfeited. It would be too easy to win by cutting down the herd."

Matt narrowed his eyes. "I don't know what you've heard about me, but I don't shoot cattle just to make my job easier."

Rufus slowly sipped his whiskey. "Actually, I've heard so many good things about you I'm starting to wonder if you hired a publicity agent. You've got a reputation as the best long-distance trail boss in the country. Even better than Rich Weaver, who Lester hired to lead his drive. Now let's see if you live up to it."

Matt knew people spoke highly of him, marveling at his dedication to his work. They never seemed to realize that he didn't have anything else.

But that was all about to change.

"I want a check for five hundred thousand dollars waiting for me at the bank in Jacksboro."

Rufus pulled open his top desk drawer. "That reminds me. I had a contract drawn up so we do everything legal. That damn IRS is always breathing down my neck."

Matt picked up the contract, leafing through the pages. Despite the legalese, he could see it clearly spelled out that Rufus would pay him the amount they'd agreed upon if Matt and his crew were the first ones across the finish line.

"Do you have a pen?"

Rufus fumbled in his drawer, then handed him one. "So when do you expect to hit Jacksboro?"

"I'm hoping to travel ten to fifteen miles a day, depending on the weather." Matt scribbled his signature across the bottom of the contract, right below Tupper's messy scrawl. "We'll drive the cattle hard for five days at a time, then graze for two. With a little luck, we should arrive at the Lazy R about a month from now. Probably mid-February."

Rufus scowled. "You'd get there a lot faster if you didn't stop to graze."

"Three hundred miles is a long way to go. Your steers would be nothing but skin and bones by the time we got to Jacksboro. If they made it that far."

"I don't give a damn about that." Rufus scowled. "I just don't want to lose."

Matt slid the contract back across the desk. "I don't intend to lose."

"Good." Rufus settled back in his chair. "Although I should warn you that Lester cheats at cards. No reason to believe he won't find a way to cheat on the trail, too."

"I'll keep my eyes open."

The rancher smirked. "'Course, I wouldn't mind if you caused Lester's cowboys a little trouble along the way. I even put a few ideas in Boyd's head that should add some fun to the trip. Did I mention he's going along?"

"So I heard." Matt stood up, planting both palms on the polished surface of Tupper's desk. "But let's get one thing straight. I don't cheat. And any man on my crew who decides to implement one of your *plans* will find himself walking barefoot back to Fort Sumner.''

Rufus chuckled. ''That's the difference between us, Radcliffe. You're honest and poor. I'm dishonest and rich. It's time you wise up, son, before you lose both the bet and the nice fat check that's already got your name on it.''

Matt had never been so tempted to walk away. Leave behind Rufus and his frivolous bet. Finding work had never been a problem before. Finding someone willing to pay him half a million dollars was another story. Especially since he was only three hundred miles away from making his dream come true.

A ranch of his very own.

He'd dreamed of it ever since he was fifteen years old, lying under the stars on his first cattle drive. Some cowboys liked the nomad life, but Matt needed roots to feel whole. Roots that had been ripped away when he was twelve years old and never replanted.

Now he was so close to his dream, he couldn't resist the offer Rufus dangled before him. Hell, why should he resist it? Rufus wouldn't miss the money. It was a stupid, meaningless bet, but if Matt didn't take the job, Rufus would find someone else to do it.

''Don't worry,'' Matt said, moving toward the door. ''I'll win your bet. And I don't intend to let Lester Hobbs or anyone else stop me.''

CHAPTER THREE

THE NEXT MORNING, Matt led his bay gelding, Jericho, out of the stable, then mounted his horse and joined his crew by the corral. He'd carefully selected them, wranglers he'd known for years whom he could trust to work hard and keep the cattle moving. He looked at them now in the predawn shadows and knew he'd chosen the best.

Cliff Donovan was his oldest friend and a cowboy with a wry sense of humor. But Cliff took his job seriously, especially now that he had a growing family to support. He was not only book smart, but cow smart, and knew how to keep a large herd under control.

Davis and Deb Gunn were a husband and wife team who could ride and rope with the best of them. They were saving money to start a dude ranch on the Wind River Range in Wyoming, where Deb had grown up. She was one of the few women he knew who looked more comfortable in a saddle than in a dress.

Arnie Schott was pushing sixty and fighting arthritis in his knees, but he still loved riding the range. The old cowboy also had good instincts when it came to river crossings and rounding up strays. He had more years of experience driving cattle than the rest of them combined.

Bud Lanigan rounded out the crew. Matt had talked him out of retirement to drive the chuck wagon and prepare the meals. Bud had grumbled about the long days ahead, but Matt could see his excitement in the avid attention he paid to the smallest details of the journey. He might not be the best cook in the country, but he'd keep them well fed over the next few weeks.

Then there was Boyd.

Matt had dragged the wiry nineteen-year-old out of bed this morning and he still looked half-asleep on top of his horse. Despite the addition of an extra hand on the drive, Matt sensed the kid would be more of a hindrance than a help.

"You awake, Tupper?" he called out.

Boyd opened his eyes. "What time is it?"

"Time to get moving." Then his gaze scanned the rest of the crew. "We've got three hundred rough miles ahead of us, but the forecast looks clear today. We'll be following the Pecos River south for the first leg of the trip. I've already gotten permission from all the landowners along the route, so we shouldn't have to worry about trespassing problems. When we reach Portales in a few days, one of us will ride into town and fetch the veterinarian. He'll check out the herd so we can cross the state line into Texas. Any questions?"

Boyd emitted a loud yawn. "I've got a question. When's breakfast?"

"You missed it," Matt replied briskly.

Bud held up a brown paper sack. "I've bagged peanut butter and jelly sandwiches for lunch if you want to eat early."

The teenager wrinkled his nose. "I hate peanut butter."

Matt swore under his breath. They hadn't even gone a mile yet, and the kid was already complaining. "Nobody here will stop you from going back to bed."

Boyd scowled, but to Matt's disappointment didn't make a move toward the bunkhouse.

The herd of one hundred Texas longhorns penned inside the corral lowed in restless anticipation, as if they sensed today was no ordinary day.

Matt looked over at Cliff, who had rounded up the lead steers and moved them to the gate. "Ready?"

"Ready," Cliff replied, then called over to Bud, who was seated on the buckboard of the chuck wagon. "Hey, save Boyd's sandwich for me. I love peanut butter."

At Matt's signal, Davis hopped off his horse and unhitched the latch. The gate swung open wide and the steers began to lumber out of the corral.

Matt raised one hand in the air, then swung it forward. "Let's ride out."

Then he took the first step toward his dream.

CALLEY STOOD in line at the Department of Motor Vehicles in Santa Fe, New Mexico. Her only lead was the phone call from White Rock. Now she just had to hope Radcliffe lived somewhere in the area, or had left a paper trail she could follow. Not that she could even be sure he was still in New Mexico. Or that he'd obtained his driver's license in this state. But she had to start somewhere.

At last she moved to the front of the line. "I'd like to know if you have any records for a Matthew C. Radcliffe. His last name is spelled R-A-D—"

"I have it," the clerk interjected, pulling a file

folder out of a wire basket. "Must be a popular guy. Another man was in here just an hour ago asking for the same information."

Her heart lurched. *Simms*. Carolyn Mulholland had told her the name of her rival. Somehow he'd gotten a step ahead of her. She inwardly chastised herself for taking time to walk her daily five miles on the treadmill in the motel's exercise room this morning. It had cost her precious time she couldn't afford, but old habits were hard to break.

Her cardiologist had stressed the importance of exercise from the first day of her diagnosis, ranking it only second to faithfully taking her medication. Which reminded her of another problem. She only had a few pills left in the bottle. Once she tracked down Matt Radcliffe, she'd have to find a pharmacy to refill her prescription. Something her mother had taken care of for as long as she could remember.

"Next," the clerk called out, breaking into Calley's thoughts. She shifted over to one side and opened the folder. Inside was a copy of Matt Radcliffe's driver's license. Her breath hitched when she saw his picture. She'd never been particularly attracted to cowboys before, but this particular cowboy could make any woman's heart beat faster. Her heart was skittering so fast in her chest, she feared it might be due to more than simple animal attraction.

Calley took a few deep breaths, then found an empty chair. She relaxed as her heart resumed its normal pace, then she took a closer look at her prey.

He had short, jet-black hair that looked like it would curl at the ends if he ever let it grow past his shirt collar. His tan complexion gave witness to long hours spent in the sun. The combination of a solid, square chin, chiseled jaw, and well-defined cheekbones made him the perfect candidate to model in *GQ* magazine. But the slight crook in his aquiline nose told her he'd probably punch any man who would suggest such an occupation.

But it was his eyes that really fascinated her.

Deep, dark-brown eyes, like chocolate melted under the warm sun. They pierced right through her and made her shift restlessly in her chair. Eyes that held his secrets and seemed to hold the power to discover hers, as well.

Not that she'd ever give him the opportunity.

Still, if he could look this good in a driver's license photograph, she didn't want to think about the effect he might have in person.

She tore her gaze from his picture and studied the statistical data. Matt Radcliffe was thirty-two years old, according to the date of birth recorded on the license. He was six feet tall and two hundred pounds, and judging by his photograph, all of it muscle. The faded chambray shirt he wore stretched taut across his broad shoulders.

Calley pulled a notepad out of her bag and jotted down the address listed on his license, 5521 Alameda Street. She handed the file back to the clerk, then hurried out the door toward her car. Finally she had a solid lead. But then, so did Bill Simms. No doubt he was well on his way to finding Matt Radcliffe while she'd been wasting time drooling over his picture.

Thirty minutes later, she was knocking on the door of 5521 Alameda Street, hoping against hope that Simms hadn't already been here. Or worse, that he and Radcliffe hadn't already left for Texas.

At last the door opened and a little girl with brown eyes blinked up at her. "Hello."

"Hi there." Calley knelt down so she would be at the little girl's eye level. The child looked to be about four or five years old, with red hair cut in a pixie style. "What's your name?"

"Bianca."

"Hello, Bianca. My name is Calley."

"You're pretty," Bianca said.

Calley smiled. "Thank you. You're very pretty, too." She wondered if this was Matt Radcliffe's child. "Is your daddy here?"

Bianca shook her head. "He's working."

"Is your name Bianca Radcliffe?" Calley asked, not able to contain her curiosity any longer.

"I'm not allowed to tell my name to strangers," Bianca replied very solemnly.

"That's right," Calley said reassuringly. "You're a very smart little girl, Bianca."

The child nodded. "I didn't tell the other man my name either."

Calley had no doubt that the other man was Bill Simms, which meant he was still one step ahead of her.

A moment later, a young blond woman, obviously pregnant, appeared at the door. "Can I help you?"

Calley straightened. "Hello, my name is Calley Graham. I'm looking for Matt Radcliffe."

"He's not here," the woman said, her expression slightly guarded.

"But he does live here?"

The woman hesitated, her hand on the door as if she might slam it shut at any moment. "Why are you looking for Matt?"

"It's...something I'm not really at liberty to discuss."

"There was a man here an hour ago looking for him, too. I don't give out personal information to strangers."

"Actually, I'm a private detective." Calley experienced an unexpected thrill at saying those words aloud. "I've been hired to find Mr. Radcliffe."

Bianca looked up at her mother. "Is Uncle Matt lost?"

Uncle Matt. If the little girl called him that, chances were good that he wasn't her father, although he could still be responsible for the child the woman was carrying. Calley briefly wondered why it mattered to her.

"No, honey," the woman said to Bianca. "He's not lost." Then she lifted her gaze back to Calley. "Matt's been good to us. I don't want to cause him any trouble."

Instinctively, Calley knew she wouldn't get anywhere with this woman unless she told her the truth. "The reason I'm looking for Mr. Radcliffe is because he's a beneficiary in a will. The sooner I find him, the sooner he can claim his inheritance."

"Oh, well that's different," the woman said with a small smile of relief. "Matt's out on a drive."

So he did live here. Calley ignored the twinge of disappointment deep inside her. "Do you mind if I wait here until he returns?"

The woman laughed. "No, I mean he's out on a cattle drive. He'll be gone for at least a month. Maybe even longer." She placed a hand on her swollen belly. "Hopefully, it will be over before I have to make a trip to the maternity ward."

"Is there any way you can contact him?" Calley asked.

"No. Although I might be able to reach my husband."

"Your husband?" Calley echoed, thoroughly confused. "Isn't Matt your husband?"

The woman laughed. "No. Matt's terminally single. Cliff Donovan is my husband. He works for Matt, although they're more like brothers than boss and employee. Matt was the best man at our wedding. He sublet his place to us a year ago. But he still uses it as his official address for mail and stuff."

A sizzle of excitement shot through Calley's veins. So Matt Radcliffe wasn't responsible for this woman's child. Her determination to find him became stronger than ever. "Tell me about this cattle drive."

MATT KNEW it was a bad sign when his horse threw a shoe before they even made it past the boundaries of the Tupper ranch. Not that he believed in all the old cowboy superstitions. But he did have a healthy respect for omens, and this one made him uneasy. Especially on the heels of Marla's curse.

At least he knew better than to relay his misgivings to the crew. Except Cliff, who had questioned the wisdom of working for a man like Tupper. In fact, Cliff had been the last one to sign on, reluctant to leave his pregnant wife and his tiny heartbreaker of a daughter. Matt regretted taking the man away from his family, but he also knew how much the Donovans could use the money. In the end, he'd left the choice up to Cliff, who had wrangled over the decision before finally agreeing to join the drive.

Fortunately, Arnie was a farrier who'd spent many years shoeing horses on the range, so the delay hadn't cost too much time. Matt easily caught up with the herd, which was moving well along the stretch of grass that paralleled Highway 20.

Bringing up the rear was Bud, driving the chuck wagon. Two extra horses were tied to the back of the wagon in case one of the working horses turned up lame. The terms of the bet made it clear that this was to be an authentic, old-fashioned cattle drive. No motor vehicles, no cellular phones or any other modern conveniences of the twentieth century. The only exception to that rule was allowing them to stock up on supplies at towns along the route.

Each cowboy carried a bedroll on the back of his saddle. Their saddlebags contained rain gear, extra clothes and personal toiletries. Pup tents were packed in the chuck wagon in case of inclement weather, along with a first-aid kit, matches, blankets, towels, soap and plenty of nonperishable food and other supplies.

Five hours after leaving the Tupper ranch near Fort Sumner, they reached the first watering hole—a small cove branching off the Pecos River. The cattle moved eagerly toward the water, some walking right into it up to their bellies.

Matt took off his cowboy hat and wiped his damp brow with his bandanna. It was going to be hot again today, which meant he'd have to slow down the drive so he didn't lose any cattle to the heat.

He looked up to see Arnie hailing him. Reining his horse around, Matt rode over to him.

"We've got a problem," Arnie said without preamble.

"What now?" Matt asked, dread churning in his stomach. "Stray cattle? A lame horse?"

"Worse," Arnie replied. "A woman."

CHAPTER FOUR

CALLEY COULDN'T believe her good luck. She'd found him. After following Katie Donovan's directions to the Tupper ranch outside of Fort Sumner, she'd simply followed the trail of cow pies until she'd caught up with the cattle drive. Not exactly the latest in high-tech tracking techniques, but it had worked.

As she slowly approached the herd in her old '82 Cadillac, she saw four men on horses turn to stare at her. Not wanting to spook either the cattle or the cowboys, she stopped her car and got out to walk the rest of the way.

A man on horseback met her halfway. Her breathing hitched when she recognized him as Matt Radcliffe. Those dark eyes were even more powerful in person than they had been in his driver's license photo.

He climbed down from his horse and walked toward her, a fantasy in faded blue denim. His square jaw was shaded with dark whiskers and his mouth was set in a firm line. When he finally reached her, he took off his cowboy hat. A gesture she found endearingly old-fashioned.

"Are you lost, ma'am?" His deep voice slid over her like smooth whiskey.

She swallowed. "Not if you're Matt Radcliffe."

. His eyes narrowed slightly. "I am."

She smiled. "Then today is your lucky day. My name is Calley Graham and I'm a private investigator with Finders Keepers out of Trueblood, Texas. You've been named as a beneficiary in Violet Mitchum's will."

Something flickered in his deep-brown eyes. Surprise? Pleasure? Pain? Calley couldn't begin to fathom the emotions swirling in those chocolate depths.

At last he said, "I think there must be some mistake."

She heard the edge in his tone but barreled ahead anyway. "I assure you there's no mistake. You're to receive one of Violet's rings and a letter she wrote to you shortly before her death."

"I'm not interested in anything Violet Mitchum had to say," he said brusquely. "Now if you'll excuse me, I have to get back to work."

Her jaw dropped as he turned around and headed back toward his horse. The man was walking away from a bequest. Possibly a very generous bequest, considering the size of the Mitchum estate.

"Wait a minute," Calley called, hurrying after him. "I don't think you understand."

Matt had already mounted his horse, his cowboy hat now shading his eyes from her. "I understand perfectly, Miss Graham. It is Miss, isn't it?"

Calley nodded. "Yes. I've never been married." She wanted to kick herself as soon as the words were out of her mouth. He didn't care about her personal life, he just wanted to know how to address her. At least she'd refrained from divulging the fact that she had only dated three men in her entire life.

And that she was still a virgin.

"Well, Miss Graham, I'm in the middle of a cattle drive at the moment. But even if I was free to take a trip to Pinto, I have absolutely no desire to go there. Or to take anything from the Mitchums."

"But what about your inheritance? It could be worth a considerable amount of money."

He hesitated for only a moment. "You can give my inheritance to a local charity or to the dog pound for all I care." He tipped his hat to her. "Good day, Miss Graham."

He rode off toward the herd, leaving her staring after him. She'd successfully tracked the man down, only to have him balk at the easy part of the job— bringing him back to Texas. Calley considered her options. She could return to Finders Keepers and inform Dylan and Lily that she'd failed. Or she could keep trying to convince Matt Radcliffe to change his mind.

It was the easiest decision she'd made in a very long time.

"THAT WOMAN IS still following us," Arnie said, riding up beside Matt.

He turned around to see Calley Graham's beat-up yellow Cadillac bouncing in the distance, easily visible by the plume of dust it left in its wake. At least she had the good sense to stay far enough behind them to keep from spooking the herd. Still, it was one more irritation in a day filled with irritations. They hadn't even come close to reaching their daily mile quota. At this rate, he'd never make it to the Lazy R in four weeks.

With a muttered curse, Matt spurred his horse forward. "Ignore her," he called back to Arnie. "She'll get bored before too long and go away."

Four hours later, Matt was still waiting for Calley to disappear. It surprised him that a woman with her delicate beauty had such tenacity. Just as it had surprised him when she'd announced her occupation. A model or a ballerina he could have believed. But a private investigator? Somehow it just didn't fit.

Just like Violet Mitchum naming him in her will didn't fit. He feared it was more out of spite than generosity. Especially when he considered his bequest. *One of Violet's rings.* He knew exactly what ring it was, and how little she'd valued it.

His mind drifted back to a day twenty-two years ago, when he'd found Violet weeping after her neighbor had stopped by to show off her new mother's ring. Violet and Charles had been unable to have children of their own, and that neighbor's visit had been like vinegar poured on an open wound. So Matt, just ten years old, had hurried up to his bedroom and retrieved his latest prize from a gumball machine: a cheap, adjustable ring with shiny fake gems glued on top. He'd solemnly presented it to Violet, telling her she could pretend to be his mother. And she'd worn it every day.

Until the fire.

He closed his eyes, still able to smell the acrid odor of charred wood. The fire had been his fault. He'd hidden in a linen closet that day to sneak a smoke of one of Charles Mitchum's big cigars. When one of the maids discovered him there, he'd made a run for it, leaving the smoldering cigar behind.

Later that night, a hysterical Violet had jerked the ring off her finger and thrown it at him, shrieking that she wasn't his mother. Violet Mitchum had made her feelings for him perfectly clear that day, and he didn't have any reason to believe those feelings had changed.

"Hey, Matt!"

He opened his eyes to see Cliff galloping toward him. The expression on his face didn't bode well.

"What's the problem?" Matt asked as Cliff reined his horse to a stop.

"It's Bud." Cliff tipped up his hat and wiped the sweat off his brow. "The chuck wagon lost a wheel about a mile back. Bud busted his wrist trying to repair it."

"Damn." Matt wheeled his horse around and rode toward the back of the herd. When he finally reached the lopsided chuck wagon, he saw the old cowboy seated on the ground, holding a wet cloth on his arm.

"What the hell happened?" Matt asked as he dismounted.

"Freak accident." Bud winced as he lifted his forearm. "I guess my reflexes ain't as good as they used to be. The axle on the wagon split as I was mounting a new wheel. Heard the bone crack and now it's swelling up something awful."

Matt nodded toward the half-empty whiskey bottle at Bud's side. "I see you've been taking something for the pain."

"There won't be any supper for you boys tonight." Bud lifted the bottle with his good hand and took a deep swig. "You'll have to make do with the beef jerky and dried apples I've got stored in the trunk."

"Don't worry about us." Matt walked to the back of the wagon, then knelt down to look at the broken axle. What he saw made his gut tighten. A neatly sawed fissure right above the splintered wooden beam. This hadn't been any accident. Someone had deliberately sabotaged the chuck wagon.

"Have you met up with anyone unusual today?" Matt asked.

Bud shook his head, then leaned against the wagon. "Just that lady who's been trailing us. But she's kept her distance."

Matt turned and looked at the Cadillac, now stopped about five hundred feet behind them. Calley Graham stepped out of the vehicle and began walking toward the chuck wagon. His gut told him she didn't have anything to do with this mess. Not only would a woman of her stature have difficulty sawing her way through solid walnut, but she'd never had the opportunity. The chuck wagon had been closed up in one of the storage sheds on Tupper's place until this morning. And Tupper was fanatical about keeping strangers out. He even had a twenty-four-hour guard at the front gate of his ranch.

So who did that leave? Marla had cursed him and the cattle drive only last night. Had she cajoled one of Tupper's ranch hands into doing the dirty deed? Or had one of Hobbs's men found a way to sabotage the chuck wagon without anyone noticing?

Matt still hadn't figured out the answer by the time the Graham woman approached him.

"What happened?" she asked, looking first at the lopsided wagon, then at Bud.

"That's just what I wanted to ask you, Miss Graham."

"Please call me Calley," she replied.

"Okay, Calley." He removed his cowboy hat. "Since you've been stalking us for the last several hours, I was wondering if you happened to see anyone hovering around the back of the wagon."

She shook her head. "It stopped three or four times, but the only person I saw was him." She pointed to Bud, who was now sucking the last drops of whiskey out of the bottle.

"Are you sure about..." His voice trailed off as the sound of an automobile engine caught his attention. A pickup truck roared toward them, kicking dust and gravel behind its tires. Several grazing steers tensed, then turned as one and bolted.

Matt swore as he jumped on his horse, hollering to the cowboys ahead of him. Fortunately, they'd seen the commotion and had positioned themselves to prevent a stampede. When Matt was certain that a catastrophe had been avoided, he wheeled his horse around and rode up to the pickup truck.

"What the hell do you think you're doing?"

The man who stepped out from behind the wheel didn't reply. Instead, he asked a question of his own. "You Matt Radcliffe?"

"Who wants to know?"

"The name is Simms. Bill Simms."

Matt saw Calley tense out of the corner of his eye. Simms wore a wrinkled blue suit and his thinning gray hair was parted just above his left ear. He had a spot of mustard on his striped tie and a weariness in his pale-gray eyes.

Matt looked from Simms to Calley. "You people seem to be under the mistaken impression that this trail ride is open to the public. I assure you that's not the case. I have work to do and you're both wasting my time."

"I have a job to do, too," Simms replied. "And that's to bring you back with me to Texas."

Matt shook his head. "Since you and Calley are so all fired anxious to see Texas, why don't you go there together and leave me the hell alone."

Simms glanced at her. "I take it you're my competition?"

"That's right," she replied evenly, holding out her hand. "I'm Calley Graham."

Simms shook it, his eyes widening. "Graham? You any relation to Walt Graham?"

She stepped back, her expression suddenly wary. "He's my father."

"I used to work with Walt. He was a hell of an investigator." Simms smiled. "I take it you're following in the old man's footsteps?"

She nodded. "I'm trying, but it seems Mr. Radcliffe isn't interested in his inheritance."

A loud snore reverberated from Bud. It reminded Matt that he had more serious problems than two cattle drive crashers. Cowboys who needed to be fed, for one. And with Bud out of commission, this drive might end before it even began.

Unless he could find a replacement.

Matt studied Bill Simms, sizing him up. The man was about Bud's age, maybe a few years younger.

The paunch and double chin told him Simms hadn't endured any strenuous physical activity in a long while. Still, beggars couldn't be choosers. And Matt was willing to settle for just about anyone if it meant winning this race.

"I'll make you a deal," Matt said to Simms over the rumble of Bud's snores. "You take over as the camp cook and chuck wagon driver until the end of the trail drive, and I'll return to Texas with you when it's over."

Simms snorted. "I can't even boil water."

"So you'll learn as you go," Matt replied, knowing the cowboys might balk at that arrangement. But what choice did he have? They'd hired on knowing they'd be roughing it for the next few weeks. Only now it looked as if their stomachs would be roughing it, too.

"Wait a minute," Calley said, her blue eyes wide. "That's not fair."

"It's business," Matt told her in a clipped tone, ignoring the twinge in his gut. He had more to think about than hurting a stranger's feelings. His ranch was waiting for him. All he had to do was earn it. "Well? Do we have a deal?"

Simms shook his head. "I'm not the outdoor type. Besides, I have a feeling you'll change your mind about the inheritance. Never known a man yet to turn free money down." He pulled a small business card out of his shirt pocket. "Give me a call when you're ready to meet with the lawyers."

When Matt refused to take the card, Simms shrugged, then walked over to Jericho and tucked it in the saddle. With a backward wave of his hand, he sauntered off toward his pickup truck.

"Hold on," Matt called after him.

Simms turned. "Change your mind already?"

"I have an injured man here," Matt replied. "Since you're headed back to civilization, can you take him to the nearest hospital?"

Simms glanced down at Bud. "He's drunk."

"He's in a lot of pain." Matt walked over to the old cowboy and gently shook him. "Time to wake up."

"Yeah…what do you want?" Bud's eyelids fluttered, then he winced. "Damn! My arm hurts like hell."

Matt carefully hefted Bud to his feet. "This man's going to take you to see a doctor."

Simms reached out to steady the inebriated cowboy, then looped Bud's good arm around his shoulder and headed for his truck. But not before giving Calley a speculative backward glance. "Take care, Miss Graham."

Calley didn't say anything until Simms had loaded Bud into the truck and driven off. Then she turned to Matt. "I'll do it."

He looked at her. "Do what?"

"I'll drive the chuck wagon. And cook the meals. And anything else you need me to do."

He smiled in spite of himself. "Forget it."

Her brow furrowed. "Why? You just offered the job to Bill Simms."

"That's because I thought he might be able to handle it."

"So can I!" She followed him, refusing to let the subject drop. "I'm an excellent cook."

"Cooking food on the trail isn't the same as puttering around in a kitchen. We don't have electric stoves or microwave ovens or dishwashers. No refrigeration, either.''

"Good. I like challenges.''

His smile widened. He had to give her credit. She was almost as stubborn as he was. ''You might like challenges, but you won't like those mules that pull the chuck wagon. They'll need to be fed and watered every day. And they'll stop when you want them to go and go when you want them to stop.''

"My grandpa raised mules on his farm,'' she countered. ''I've always been good with animals.''

He turned around to face her. ''The answer is no.''

"That's not fair.'' She took a deep breath. ''At least give me a chance to prove myself. And if I can do the job for the duration of the cattle drive, then you'll come back to Texas with me. Just like you offered to do with Simms.''

Matt considered her proposal. More than likely she wouldn't last one day, much less the month it was going to take them to reach the Lazy R. Calley Graham had no idea what she was volunteering for. Heat and dust and flies. Not to mention sleeping on a hard wagon bed every night and washing in an icy stream.

Still, her offer might buy him a little time to figure out another solution to this unexpected problem. It would take him and the boys the rest of the day to round up the herd and rig up a new axle for the chuck wagon. A decent supper would be a just reward for their first hard day on the trail.

"If I agree,'' he began, noting the spark of hope that lit her blue eyes, ''you'll have to follow through with your part of the bargain. All the meals will be your responsibility, as well as driving the wagon and caring for the mules. No one else will have time to help you out."

"I can do it," she vowed.

He shook his head, certain he was making a mistake. But what choice did he have at this point? "You'll have to leave your car here."

"Not a problem," she said evenly.

His eyes narrowed. "Why is this so important to you?"

Calley hesitated for a whisper of a second. "I believe in living up to my responsibilities. I took on the job of bringing you back to Texas and I intend to see it through—no matter what I have to do."

Matt couldn't argue with that. "We'll be camping here tonight. I guess you can use Bud's supplies since he won't be needing them now. His bedroll is inside the wagon."

She nodded. "All right. But I just want to make sure we're clear. If I can do the job until the trail drive is over, you'll let me take you back to Texas for Violet Mitchum's memorial service."

"I give you my word, Miss Graham," he said solemnly. He didn't add that she'd never be able to tough it out. Or that he'd rather walk barefoot through a thick field of cockleburs than return to the Mitchum house again.

She held out her hand. "Shall we shake on it?"

He took her hand in his, surprised at the softness and warmth of her skin. Her small fingers seemed fragile in his grasp, although her grip was surprisingly strong. Even more surprising was the virile reaction he had to her touch. Matt realized too late that he might have made a huge mistake.

"One more thing," he said, seeking a reason to keep holding her hand. He didn't like the need she stirred in him. Or the way her blue eyes made him want to move closer. "If you can't hack it, then you walk away. I don't want you getting hurt or putting yourself in danger because you're in over your head."

She gazed up at him with an enigmatic gleam in her blue eyes. "There's one thing you should know about me, Mr. Radcliffe. I've dedicated my life to living dangerously."

CHAPTER FIVE

CALLEY HADN'T exactly lied. She did know how to cook. It had been one of the few hobbies available to her over the last ten years that her mother hadn't deemed too exhausting or stressful. Her specialty was Chinese cooking, but there wasn't a wok in sight. Even worse, she'd never cooked over an open fire before. Or faced such an interesting array of ingredients.

"Dried beans...dried corn...dried onions," she read aloud, sorting through the boxes of food stacked inside the chuck wagon. "Potato flakes...powdered milk...powdered eggs."

At least contemplating tonight's menu was easier than dealing with those balky mules. Matt had unhitched them from the chuck wagon before beginning the repairs. Samson and Delilah seemed to appreciate the sugar cubes she'd discovered, and Samson had christened her with a snort from his nose.

It was true her grandfather had raised mules on his farm, but she'd failed to mention that he'd sold that farm before she was born. Telling the truth would have gotten her a one-way ticket back to Texas. She knew Matt was already regretting his decision to let her join the cattle drive. Now it was up to her to prove that she was the right woman for the job.

She climbed out of the back of the chuck wagon,

half wishing she could dial up for takeout on her cellular phone. But she'd left it in the car after Matt had told her that such items were forbidden on this drive. At least he'd let her bring her suitcase.

Her Cadillac looked lonely and abandoned in the fading twilight. Her first car, it had cost her five hundred dollars and almost cleared out her meager savings account. Her mother had been furious at the purchase, claiming a person with Calley's condition shouldn't endanger herself or others by getting behind the wheel. But Calley had stood firm, causing the first rift between the two of them. A rift that had now widened into the Grand Canyon.

The odds were high that the car would be gone by the time the cattle drive was over. But hopefully by then she'd be working for Finders Keepers and could afford a new one. Maybe a sporty red convertible. Or an SUV with all the options. She smiled to herself, realizing how nice it was to have a fantasy that actually had a chance of coming true.

She grabbed a spade from a hook on the back of the wagon, then walked to the center of the camp and began digging a small pit. Then she roamed the camp, gathering twigs and brush to fuel a fire. By the time she got a blaze going, she'd wasted an entire book of matches.

Now came the hard part. The eternal question of women everywhere: What to make for supper.

"Howdy."

Calley looked up from the fire to see a tall, strapping woman with slightly buck teeth and a welcoming smile. "Hello."

"I'm Deb Gunn." She held out her hand, her fingers lined with old scars and rough with calluses.

"Calley Graham." As they shook hands, Calley realized she hadn't noticed there was a woman among Matt's crew. Deb disguised her figure well in baggy blue denim jeans, a cotton shirt two sizes too big, and a bulky bandanna tied around her neck. She wore her straw cowboy hat low over her brow, her dusky brown curls peeking out under the brim.

"Nice to meet you, Calley." Deb waved off a fly. "I have to admit it's nice to have another woman along on the trail."

"I'm thrilled to be here," she replied honestly. "Although this is all a little new to me."

"Well, if you need a hand, just give me a holler. I've spent more time around cattle than I have around people, so I know how to survive on the range. And I'll tell Davis to keep an eye out for you, too."

"Davis?"

"My husband." She pointed to the skinny cowboy with the goatee busily setting up a pup tent on the edge of the camp. He reminded Calley of Festus from the old *Gunsmoke* series.

"I'd appreciate the help," she told Deb, "although I'm not sure your boss will like it."

Deb smiled. "Is Matt giving you a hard time already? That man's got a knack for driving pretty women away. My personal theory is that he's scared one of them is going to lasso him and drag him to the altar. Just like I did with Davis."

"I just want to drag him to Texas," Calley said, then explained her reason for joining the cattle drive.

"I always did admire a woman who goes after what she wants."

Calley gave a weary sigh. "You may change your mind after you eat my cooking. I've never cooked anything outdoors before and I'm not exactly sure how it's going to turn out.''

"Well, you don't have to worry about me. I've got an iron stomach. And Davis won't hold it against you. Hell, he still asked me out after I fixed him my special chili and he had to have his stomach pumped.''

Deb pointed to a tall red-haired cowboy brushing down a black horse. "That's Cliff. He's a gentleman through and through, so he won't give you any trouble. And I'm sure Arnie's suffered through plenty of lousy cooks in all the years he's been on the trail. Now, Boyd's another story.''

"Which one is Boyd?" Calley asked,

"The skinny kid with the silver spoon in his mouth.'' She pointed toward the young man riding along the edge of the herd. "He's Rufus Tupper's nephew and he's been whining all day about missing breakfast. But none of us pay him any mind, so don't you either.''

"So the only one I really need to impress is Matt.''

Deb grinned. "I think you've already done that, Calley. I saw the way he was looking at you earlier.''

Her cheeks grew hot. "I'm not so sure about that.''

"I am. And I just have one piece of advice for you.''

"What's that?''

"Well, men are a little bit like mules. Stubborn as hell and never headed in the right direction. Sometimes you got to sweet-talk them into submission. And if that doesn't work, just give 'em a good kick in the butt.''

Calley bit back a smile. "I'll keep that in mind.''

"And don't worry about supper tonight. I'll have

a talk with the boys and tell them to be on their best behavior.''

"Thank you, Deb.''

"We women have got to stick together.'' Then she turned and started hollering instructions to her husband, who had the tent halfway up.

Calley watched her walk away, noting the way her knees seemed to bow just a little. If a seasoned veteran like Deb thought she could handle this job, maybe she could do it after all. Pushing up her shirtsleeves, Calley headed back to the chuck wagon, determined to make a supper Matt Radcliffe would never forget.

AN HOUR LATER, Calley wasn't so optimistic. The crew had quit work and were now each staking out a place for the night. She'd taken another quick inventory of the chuck wagon, noting the smoked hams hanging from the ribbed awning and the small barrels of flour, coffee and sugar. She'd found a box of soft tortilla shells inside an old trunk, along with several bags of assorted dried fruit.

Unfortunately she hadn't come across any cookbooks, recipes, or cans of ready-to-serve spaghetti. Which meant she was going to have to wing it.

"Stick with something simple,'' she muttered to herself. "Like ham and beans.'' The problem was, the white beans were hard as a rock. The only beans she'd ever cooked had come in a can.

With a fervent hope that she was doing the right thing, she dumped the beans into one of the large cast-iron pots, added some water, then placed it on the portable grate she'd set up over the fire. While the beans cooked, she chopped up a chunk of smoked ham, then added that to the pot, too.

Matt rode up just as she was taking a peek under the lid. It didn't look good.

"Supper almost ready?"

"It'll be a little while yet." She replaced the lid, then looked up at him. He sat on his horse as if he'd been born there, one hand absently reaching out to pat its long neck.

"What's her name?" Calley asked.

Matt's brow furrowed. "Who?"

"Your horse."

A smile tipped up one corner of his mouth. "Jericho. Although she is actually a he. A gelding to be exact."

"What's a gelding?" she asked, then realized too late she'd let her city-girl roots show.

"It's a male horse that's been..." he hesitated, as if searching for the right word. "Let me put it this way. Jericho will always be a bachelor."

"Oh." Then she blinked as a slow flush burned up her neck. *"Oh."*

His smile widened, then he turned his horse back toward the herd. "Just ring the bell when supper's ready."

"I'll do that," she replied, awed by the way his smile transformed his face. For that brief moment, he'd looked friendly. Even charming. A trait he obviously wanted to keep to himself, judging by the way he spurred his horse.

Calley sighed, then sniffed. Something smelled funny. She turned toward the fire and saw black smoke seeping out of the lid. She rushed over to the pot and grabbed the handle, dropping it a split second later.

"Damn," she muttered, tears stinging her eyes as she plunged her hand into the bucket of water she'd dipped out of the stream earlier. She watched helplessly as smoke rolled out of the pot. When the pain subsided enough for her to remove her hand from the water, she grabbed a potholder and lifted the pot from the flames.

"Oh, no," she moaned, staring down into the blackened lump of beans and ham. She probably wouldn't be able to fool Matt with this dish. In fact, she'd be lucky if he didn't order her back to her car and out of his sight.

She looked out over the herd, glimpsing Matt's black cowboy hat in the distance. At this moment she wanted to do more than keep her job. She wanted to prove to him that she wasn't some helpless city woman.

Now she just had to figure out a way to do it.

THE SUN HAD disappeared below the horizon by the time Matt finally heard the clang of the dinner bell. His stomach had been growling for the last hour especially since Boyd had been reciting the long list of his favorite meals for anyone who would listen.

Matt's mouth watered as he walked toward the campsite to wash up. His favorite meal was chicken-fried steak with mashed potatoes and thick, cream gravy. He hadn't eaten homemade chicken-fried steak since he was twelve years old. It had been Violet Mitchum's special recipe. She'd always made it for his birthday, and sometimes for no special occasion at all.

Just to make him happy.

Matt mentally shook himself. He didn't want to think about Violet. He hadn't thought about her for a very long time—until Calley showed up, bringing all those memories rushing back. Matt couldn't afford to get caught up in the past. Not when he was so close to finally realizing the future he'd dreamed of for so long.

Cliff walked up alongside him, matching his stride. "Do you smell something funny?"

"You mean besides one hundred head of cattle up close and personal?"

"That's nothing new for us." Cliff sniffed the air. "This smells more like…a really bad Mexican restaurant."

As they moved closer to the chuck wagon, the odor hit Matt's nostrils. It wasn't offensive exactly, just very unusual.

By the time Matt had cleaned up, the rest of the crew was already seated on upturned crates around the fire. Calley still stood at the chuck wagon, where a serving board hinged to one side held a large pot and a stack of tin plates.

When Matt finally reached her, he couldn't help but notice the rosy blush in her cheeks and the sparkle in her too blue eyes. If it wasn't such a ridiculous notion, he'd say she was having the time of her life.

"Hope you're hungry," she said, pushing a plate into his hands.

Matt looked down at three rolled-up tortilla shells. "Tacos?"

"Not exactly." She poured him a steaming cup of coffee. "I call them Calley's Special Trail Wraps. I guarantee you've never had anything like them before.''

He found himself staring at her. Wondering once more what a woman as attractive and vivacious as Calley Graham was doing on a dusty cattle drive with a bunch of tired cowboys.

He glanced at the rest of the crew, now circling the fire. He could hear the low rumble of their voices, but couldn't discern their words. So far, none of them had returned for a second helping of Calley's Special Trail Wraps.

''I'll grab a crate for you,'' she said, climbing into the back of the chuck wagon.

He watched her, appreciating the way her jeans molded to her shapely backside. Then he looked away, chiding himself for giving her this job. She was a distraction. One he definitely didn't need.

They walked together to the campfire, Calley carrying the crate and Matt carrying his dinner plate. The unusual odor emanating from it only increased his apprehension.

''Samson and Delilah seem to like me,'' she said, referring to the mules.

''Let's hope they remember that when it's time to move out tomorrow morning.''

''What time should I set the alarm clock?''

''Four a.m.''

She blinked. ''Does that seem a little early to you? I mean, the cattle need their rest.''

He smiled in spite of himself. ''The cook has to have breakfast ready and waiting by the time the cowboys roll out of their bedrolls. We'll break camp at sun-up.''

She set the crate down beside Cliff. "Then four o'clock it is."

Matt took a seat, then picked up a wrap and bit off a man-size bite. Several different flavors assaulted his tongue at once. Charred meat, Tabasco sauce, and some waxy, pasty substance that made him want to spit it back out. Instead, he forced himself to swallow, then looked up at Calley.

"Well?" she asked, an expectant expression on her face.

"What exactly is this?"

"My own version of blackened refried beans. It's sort of a combination Cajun-Mexican dish."

His gaze circled the crew, who all had their eyes fixed on their plates. Their *empty* plates. Then he looked at the fire. The blaze was fed by not only twigs and brush, but several charred remnants of supper.

He took a sip of coffee, ignoring the burn on his tongue. Then he set his plate on the ground. "You told me you could cook. In fact, I believe your words were, *I'm an excellent cook.*"

Her blue eyes turned bluer. "You don't like it?"

The disappointment in her voice ate at him worse than the pasty glop he'd just swallowed. This was why he couldn't have a woman like Calley on a cattle drive. He had to worry too much about hurting her feelings. Matt wasn't a man to tiptoe around the truth, but at this moment he'd rather eat a dozen of Calley's Special Trail Wraps than admit how incredibly awful they tasted.

Cliff handed her his plate. "It's the best meal I've had in a long time, Miss Graham."

Her face lit up. "Thank you! And please call me Calley."

Matt watched in amazement as Arnie and Davis followed suit. Seemed like he wasn't the only one wary of bruising a lady's tender feelings.

Boyd spoke next, motivated by a sharp elbow jab in the ribs from Deb. "Thank you for the supper," he sputtered. "It was…delicious."

Calley beamed.

"You're welcome, Boyd."

Deb winked at Matt. "She's definitely a keeper."

Matt cleared his throat. "I don't really care for spicy food."

Cliff stood up. "Then let's get on with the evening's entertainment." He pushed his crate toward Matt, then rolled up the sleeve of his right arm. "Are you ready to take me on?"

Matt ignored the hollow ache in his stomach and began rolling up his sleeve. "Anytime, anyplace, Donovan. Name your terms."

"Winner gets to eat the chocolate chip cookies the wife packed in my saddle bag." Then he grinned. "Loser has to help Calley with the dishes."

"What's going on?" Calley asked, her brow furrowed in confusion.

"They're arm wrassling," Deb informed her. "Been doing it forever."

Matt knelt on the ground, then placed his elbow on the flat surface of the upturned crate. "And I'm ahead with 348 wins."

"And 298 losses," Cliff added, positioning his elbow on the crate. "Get ready to make it 299."

"In your dreams, Donovan." They hooked their thumbs together and wrapped their fingers tightly around each other's hand.

"On your mark," Davis said, acting as the self-appointed referee, "get set...go!"

The corded muscles stood out in Matt's neck and along his jaw as he fought to hold his arm upright. Cliff was slim, but very strong. And it didn't help to have Calley standing right in his line of vision.

"Give it up, Matt," Cliff said, his voice low enough for only the two of them to hear.

"I could sit here all night," Matt replied with a smile. He edged Cliff's arm closer to the crate surface.

Cliff glanced at Calley, then back at Matt. "Oh? Are you enjoying the view?"

He scowled as Cliff levered his arm back to an upright position. "Maybe you'd better stop talking and save your strength for washing dishes."

His friend grinned. "Did I hit a nerve, cowboy?"

"I sure do love Katie's chocolate chip cookies," Matt said, his arm starting to shake as he put all his strength into it."

"Maybe Calley could give you something even sweeter," Cliff taunted, "like a kiss under the stars."

Matt's arm hit the crate with a thud. "Damn."

"Looks like I'm the winner." Cliff stood up and waved his arms over his head like a boxer. "The new, undisputed champion in the arm wrestling arena."

"You cheated," Matt muttered, unable to stop a smile at Cliff's antics.

"All's fair in love and arm wrestling." Then he picked up the stack of empty plates on the ground and handed them to Matt with a wink. "You can thank me later."

Punching him later seemed a lot more likely. Not one to welch on a bet, he walked over to the chuck wagon, where Calley had already dumped the water she'd heated over the fire into a plastic dishpan.

She smiled as he approached. "Have you ever had one of those days when everything just seemed to go your way?"

"Not for quite a while," he replied, dumping the dirty plates into the dishwater. *And definitely not today.*

"It's so beautiful out here." She looked up into the night sky, now dotted with silvery stars. "It makes me think of that song."

Matt picked up a washcloth, then looked up into the sky. "What song?"

A blush suffused her cheeks. "Oh, it's silly, really. A song from a children's movie. 'Somewhere Out There.' About a mouse who believes there's someone else looking at the same bright star. Someone meant just for him."

Their gazes fell and met at the same moment, causing a ripple of uneasiness to prickle over his skin. He knew the song. Cliff's daughter, Bianca, had sung it over and over again when she'd tagged along on a trip to pick up some prize bulls in Idaho.

"Do you know it?" she asked softly.

"Yes." He cleared his throat, then plunged his hands into the tepid dishwater. He quickly washed the plates while she wiped them dry, the silence now heavy between them. Calley Graham was having an odd effect on him.

One he didn't like a bit.

"More coffee before I throw it out?" she asked, holding up the pot.

"No, thanks." He handed her the last plate, then dried his hands on a dish towel. So much for his earlier edict that she'd have to handle all her duties by herself. "I need to check the herd before we bunk down for the night."

"Where do you want me to sleep?"

For some reason, that innocent question caused his body to tighten in an extremely uncomfortable way. He backed away from her, stumbling over a rock on the ground. He regained his balance, then picked up the rock and threw it into the darkness. "You should be able to make some room on the floor of the chuck wagon. Then you don't have to worry about snakes or other critters crawling over you as you sleep."

Including one mixed-up cowboy.

"Good night, Matt," she called as he turned to walk away.

He didn't slow his stride. "Night."

It wasn't until he reached the herd that he realized the worst part. Calley had made it through the first day. And she didn't seem to be having any second thoughts about staying. Probably because she already had the entire crew on her side. Still, she hadn't yet experienced a full day on a cattle drive. He smiled as he untied his bedroll from his saddle.

No doubt about it. Tomorrow, Calley Graham was in for a few surprises.

CHAPTER SIX

CALLEY JUMPED as a loud clanging sounded in her ear. Then she reached out her hand and batted the alarm clock next to her head.

"Five more minutes," she murmured, turning onto her back. Her very stiff back. She winced as she arched her spine, trying to work out the knots. Then the low of a steer sounded in the distance. She opened her eyes to the pitch-black night.

The cattle drive. The bargain. The hard wooden belly of the chuck wagon underneath her. It all came rushing back into her sleep-numbed brain.

Stars twinkled at her through the keyhole opening of the chuck wagon. Calley stood up, then gathered up the bedroll, hitting her elbow against a cast-iron skillet hanging beside her.

"Crap," she whispered, then realized she didn't need to be so quiet. With the cowboys still asleep, no one could hear her.

She stumbled over a crack in the floorboards and hit her knee sharply on a storage trunk. Muttering an oath, she fished around the top shelf for a book of matches. How in the world did Matt Radcliffe expect her to make coffee in the dark of night?

She finally found them, then turned and headed out of the chuck wagon, smacking her forehead on one of the smoked hams hanging from the top of the wagon.

She'd gathered plenty of brush for last night's fire, so it didn't take her long to start a small blaze under the iron grate. Then she retrieved the clean coffeepot from the chuck wagon and headed toward the stream. Something slithered in the tall grass in front of her, making Calley jump two feet in the air.

She stopped and looked carefully around her, unable to see much of anything in the dark. In the distance, she could make out the vague shapes of the cattle. And the Gunns' pup tent under a lone mesquite tree. The lumps stretched out near the campfire must be the rest of the crew.

Calley turned back toward the stream, tentatively sticking her foot out and dipping it in the grass. She had no desire to interrupt the sleep of a coiled rattlesnake or some other wild animal.

With one slow, tedious step at a time she moved toward the stream, her eyes glued on the ground in front of her. The steady gurgle of running water soothed her nerves a little and she had to admit the predawn morning was incredibly peaceful. It was almost hard to believe that somewhere there were bustling cities full of all-night diners and honking taxicabs. Places with airplanes and buses and trains running twenty-four hours a day. At one time, the West had been exactly like this place, with nothing but the rustle of grass to break the silence. It was exactly the same here as it had been one hundred years ago. Perhaps even five hundred years ago. She looked up at the stars, wondering who else had looked at them from this very same spot.

"Good morning."

Calley yelped and spun around, her heart pounding in her chest. Matt Radcliffe sat up on his horse not five feet behind her. "Oh, it's you."

He cocked a brow. "Expecting someone else?"

"Of course not." She placed one hand on her chest and took a slow deep breath. "I wasn't expecting anyone at this hour. What are you doing up?"

"We take turns on nightshift to watch the herd."

"You mean you didn't sleep at all?"

"A few hours after supper."

She tilted her head up at him. "Why do you have to stay up all night. Afraid of rustlers?"

A smile tipped up one corner of his mouth. "You've been watching too many westerns on television."

Calley smiled. "I grew up on *Gunsmoke* reruns."

She didn't tell him that there'd been little else for her to do after her heart condition had been diagnosed. Forbidden from attending school or participating in any extracurricular activities such as sports or even 4-H club, Calley had turned to television. It had been her only form of escape.

"The main reason we patrol the herd at night is to prevent any cattle from wandering off. Most of them are content to stay put after traveling that many miles. But I don't want to waste daylight looking for strays."

"Where exactly are we headed?" she asked suddenly realizing how very little she knew about this cattle drive. Or the man in charge of it. When Finders Keepers had hired her to find him, they'd just given her a glimpse of his past. She had no idea what had made him the man he was today. Strong. Stubborn. Sexy. With a touch of old-fashioned chivalry thrown in that reminded her a little of another Matt. Sheriff Matt Dillon from *Gunsmoke*.

"The Lazy R ranch just west of Jacksboro, Texas."

"Deb told me this cattle drive is part of a bet made by, Boyd's uncle, Rufus Tupper."

He nodded. "A bet I intend to win."

She studied him for a moment.

"Why is that so important to you?"

He hesitated. "Because if I win, Tupper will pay me enough money to buy a ranch of my own and I won't have to work for fools like him anymore."

She took the lid off the coffeepot, then bent down at the edge of the stream and allowed the crystal clear water to flow inside. "Were you born a cowboy, Matt?"

"Not exactly." He didn't say anything for a long moment. "Although I was raised on a horse ranch."

She waited for him to elaborate, but instead he turned Jericho around and headed back to the herd. "Let me know when that coffee's ready."

Calley watched him ride off, wondering if she'd said something to offend him. She'd never met a man of so few words, but then, she hadn't met many men in her life. Certainly not any as intriguing as Matt Radcliffe.

After she set the coffeepot on the fire grate to percolate, she retrieved a tattered cookbook she'd discovered in the bottom of one of the storage trunks last night. It looked at least fifty years old, but she couldn't confirm a publication date because the copyright page had been torn out.

The cookbook was chock-full of recipes for life on the trail. Dishes like Son-of-a-Gun Stew, Vinegar Pie and Grits-n-Gravy. For breakfast she'd selected a simple dish that looked hearty enough to make up for last night's meager offering.

She hauled a Dutch oven from the chuck wagon and set it on the grate next to the coffeepot. Then she dumped in chunks of bacon, the fat sizzling and sending a savory aroma into the morning air. Tears stung her eyes as she chopped a bowl full of onions and added them to the pot. Next, she peeled two dozen potatoes, slicing them thin and layering them on top of the onions and bacon. Then she set the lid on top and let the fire do the rest of the work.

A while later, Boyd walked up to the campfire, wearing only blue jeans and cowboy boots. "Something smells damn good."

"It'll be ready soon." She poured him a cup of coffee. "I want to thank you for pretending you liked my supper last night. I hope this morning you won't have to lie when you tell me it's wonderful."

A flush crawled up Boyd's cheeks. "Cliff gave me some of his wife's cookies, so it wasn't like I had to starve or anything. Besides, it was fun to see that look on Radcliffe's face when all of us started to rave about your cooking."

Calley used a pot holder to lift the lid of the Dutch oven and give the contents a stir. "Are you enjoying the cattle drive?"

He grinned at her. "I am now."

"Boyd!" Matt strode up to the campfire, a scowl on his face. "Go put a shirt on. We've got enough hardships on this drive without having to watch you strut around half-naked."

Boyd's flush deepened as he glanced at Calley. "Yes, sir."

After he walked away, Matt turned to her. "Is there a problem?"

"Yes. And I think it's you."

He pointed to the east, where the sun was barely peeking over the horizon "It's almost time to break camp. The boys are ready. The cattle are ready. Hell, even the mules look ready. The only thing that isn't ready is you."

"Is that why you bit Boyd's head off?"

A muscle flexed in his jaw. "I think you're distracting my crew."

She reached for the coffeepot and poured him a cup. "And I think you're suffering from an empty stomach and not enough sleep."

"I wish it was that simple," he muttered, then took the cup from her and blew on the steaming coffee. "Maybe we should start over."

"Okay," she said with a smile. "Good morning, Matt."

He gave her a reluctant smile. "Good morning, Calley."

She lifted the lid off the Dutch oven. "Breakfast is ready if you're hungry."

"I'm starved." But he wasn't looking at the food she dished up. He was looking at her. Then the rest of the crew ambled over to the campfire and Matt turned and took a seat on one of the crates.

Calley dished up full plates for everyone, serving herself last. Pride welled up within her after she took the first bite.

"It's delicious," she announced, unable to keep the surprise out of her voice.

Everyone else was too busy chewing to reply. For

the first time, Calley believed she might be able to pull this off.

"Let's roll out," Matt said, handing her his empty plate.

"I need to wash dishes first." She removed the Dutch oven and coffeepot from the grate.

"There's no time," he replied. "You can do it when we make camp tonight."

She frowned down at the scorch marks in the bottom of the Dutch oven. "Do you have any idea how hard this pot and the rest of these dishes will be to clean by then?"

"That's not my problem." A hopeful gleam lit his eyes. "It won't be your problem either, if you decide to go back where you came from."

Calley had known from the beginning that Matt didn't want her here, but his remark stung anyway. She'd wanted to prove to him she could handle this job. *Any job.* Obviously, it was going to take more than one good breakfast to do it.

She forced a smile. "That's all right. I'll manage."

"Suit yourself."

He walked away and Calley had to resist the urge to throw the coffeepot at his head. She was probably just tired, too. Sleeping in a strange bedroll, on the hard floor of a strange chuck wagon, in a strange state, wasn't exactly conducive to a good night's sleep.

But it was the most excitement she'd had in a very long time.

Calley dumped the dirty dishes in an empty crate, then hauled it to the chuck wagon. After she'd gathered all her supplies, she reached for her purse and dug out the prescription bottle she'd carried with her for too many years to remember. She popped the familiar red-and-white capsule into her mouth, then washed it down with the last of her lukewarm coffee.

She had no intention of letting a bunch of dirty dishes, a cantankerous cowboy or a bum heart keep her from having the time of her life.

MATT WAITED until the cattle were moving before he rode up beside Boyd. "We need to have a talk."

"Talk away," Boyd said, holding the reins loosely in his hands.

"This is a cattle drive, not a cotillion. If you want to flirt with the ladies, wait until we arrive in Jacksboro. I have neither the time nor the inclination to monitor a romance on the range."

Boyd stuck out his lower lip. "I don't recall asking for your help, Radcliffe. For your information, I've had plenty of experience with women. And as long as I do my job, I don't think my love life is any of your business."

"Everything on this cattle drive is my business. And love doesn't belong on the range."

Boyd smirked. "Then why do Davis and Deb sleep in a pup tent when the rest of us sleep under the stars? Maybe they need this love on the range lecture, too."

"Just stay away from Calley," Matt said, his patience reaching the breaking point. "And keep a better eye on the perimeter. You let too many steers get past you yesterday."

Boyd's mouth thinned. "I'm new at this, you know. So is Calley. That's why we get along so good. And if you don't like it, you can just…" His voice trailed off.

"I can just what?" Matt asked, itching for a reason to send Boyd back to his uncle.

"Forget it."

"I think you're forgetting something." He spoke low and even, determined not to let Boyd Tupper make him lose his temper. Especially over a woman. "I'm the trail boss on this drive. My word is law."

He swallowed. "And if the lady comes to me?"

Matt snorted. "That isn't going to happen."

"We'll see," Boyd muttered under his breath as he wheeled his horse away from Matt. "We'll just see about that."

CHAPTER SEVEN

"HE TURNED you down?" Dylan Garrett sat in his office at Finders Keepers, keeping one eye on the clock on the wall. His guest was due to arrive soon.

Bill Simms leaned back in his chair. "That's right. Matt Radcliffe doesn't care about Violet Mitchum's will or any bequest she might have left him."

"I thought the hard part would be finding him," Dylan mused. "Not bringing him back to Pinto."

"The guy's got a real chip on his shoulder. I almost felt bad for leaving Miss Graham there with him."

Dylan blinked. "Calley found him, too?"

"About five minutes before I did," Bill admitted. "But he'd already turned her down when I showed up. I guess she decided to stick around awhile and see if she could persuade him to change his mind. But I've been around his kind before. Too mule-headed for their own good, if you know what I mean."

He knew exactly what Bill meant. Dylan had been described as mule-headed a time or two himself. Not that he was anywhere near as stubborn as his twin sister. Fortunately that family trait was paying off for Lily. Her determination to keep her baby had resulted in encouraging news at her last doctor's visit. Only a few more weeks of bedrest and she might be able to resume most of her normal activities.

"Sure was strange seeing her again," Bill said.

Dylan realized he hadn't been paying attention. "Who?"

"Calley Graham. I met her about ten years back at a benefit. Her dad Walt Graham and I were both cops on the police force. He took about a year's leave when his daughter got so sick. I remember covering more than one shift for him." A smile haunted his mouth. "I haven't seen the Grahams in almost a decade. Seeing Calley again brings back a lot of old memories."

Dylan momentarily forgot about his real reason for asking Bill to come here. Calley Graham seemed perfectly healthy to him. "What happened to her?"

"A dud ticker. She was right as a raindrop until she turned fifteen. Then one day she keeled over and they had her hooked up to a bunch of machines in the hospital before the day was out."

"Are you telling me she has a heart condition?"

"Yeah, the name for it is some fifty-dollar word that I can't spell, much less pronounce. Considering her prognosis at the time, I figured she'd be dead by now."

A knock sounded on the door, then his office assistant stuck her head inside. "Sebastian Cooper is here to see you."

Dylan nodded. "Give me a few minutes, Carolyn, then send him in."

Bill Simms started to rise.

"I'd like you to stay," Dylan said, waving him back into the chair. "That is, if you're interested in doing some more work for me. I'll even pay you this time."

Bill laughed, then shook his head. "I don't know.

I've decided I'm too old to be traipsing all over the country.''

"This case is local. And sensitive. I think a former officer with the San Antonio PD is just the man for the job.''

"What exactly do you want me to do?'' Bill asked, settling back in his chair

"There's a man named Sebastian Cooper outside. His wife has been missing for over a year. He claims he wants to find her, but I've got reason to believe he's connected to J. B. Crowe's crime ring. So her life may be in danger.''

"Crowe's in prison, isn't he?''

Dylan nodded. "Yes, but according to Zach Logan, Crowe's got his second in command running things on the outside. A thug named Luke Silva.''

"So you want me to find the dirt on Cooper?''

"Yes. You could start by searching his personal and business finances. See if anything suspicious turns up.''

"Then what?''

"Sniff around Luke Silva. I want to know if they've met or done any business deals together.''

"Anything else?''

Dylan nodded. "Sebastian wants Finder Keepers to find his wife. I plan to tell him I'm bringing you in on the case.''

"Okay. Where do you want me to look for her?''

"Nowhere.''

Bill blinked. "Come again.''

Dylan studied Simms, wondering how much he could trust him. The last thing he wanted to do was put Julie in any more danger. "At this point, I want you to agree to take the case, but not do any actual investigation.''

''And if he wants a progress report?''

''Phony up some leads. Like possible sightings in different states.''

Simms smiled. ''You want to send him on a wild-goose chase.''

''For now.''

The door opened and Sebastian Cooper walked in.

Dylan noted the new lines around his eyes and the sallowness in his complexion. The last few months had taken a toll on his old friend. He'd almost feel sorry for Sebastian if he didn't know the hell the man had put Julie through.

Dylan made the introductions. ''Sebastian, this is Bill Simms. I've added him to the team to find Julie. He's a former police officer and a top-notch investigator.''

Sebastian shook Bill's hand, then moved to the liquor cabinet and poured himself a generous whiskey. ''Nothing new to report?''

For one brief moment Dylan was tempted to tell him the truth. *I've seen your wife, Sebastian. She's frail and beautiful and scared as hell. Of you. And I've seen your son—a son you don't deserve.*

''Not yet,'' Dylan hedged. ''But the case could turn around at any time.''

Sebastian swore viciously under his breath, then downed the whiskey. ''Where the hell is she? A woman can't just disappear off the face of the earth. Especially a woman with a baby.''

Bill pulled a notepad and pencil from his shirt pocket. ''Can I ask you a few questions, Mr. Cooper?''

Sebastian refilled his glass, then turned to Dylan. "Haven't you already filled him in?"

"I prefer to get my facts directly from the source," Bill replied, licking the tip of the pencil. "How old is your wife?"

"Thirty." Sebastian moved to a brown leather armchair and sat down. "She's got blue eyes and long blond hair."

Her hair is brown now, Dylan thought to himself. *And cut short so no one will recognize her.* She'd turned her blue eyes brown with a pair of colored contact lenses. And she was thinner than ever before. Thinner than a woman who had just given birth should be.

Bill's pencil scratched across the notepad. "How about her background?"

Sebastian tugged on the tie around his neck. "She was born in Wisconsin and raised on a dairy farm. But I've already contacted her parents and they haven't seen her. Nobody's seen or heard from her since the car-jacking."

After a few more notes, Bill looked up at Sebastian. "When exactly did the car-jacking take place?"

"Last January. Right after New Year's. And they found...blood in the car." He took a deep shuddering breath. "I just want my wife back."

Dylan's eyes narrowed on Sebastian. The lying son of a bitch deserved to have his capped teeth knocked out. There was only one person to blame for Julie's disappearance, and that was Sebastian himself.

"Perfectly understandable, Mr. Cooper." Bill closed his notebook and stuffed it back into his pocket. "I'll take whatever steps are necessary to see that this job is done right."

Sebastian stood up and turned to Dylan. "Thanks for all your help, buddy. I really do appreciate it."

"You know I'd do anything for Julie," Dylan replied solemnly. "Bringing her safely home is my top priority."

CALLEY ACHED everywhere. Her hands burned from holding the thick leather harness reins. Her feet hurt from the number of times she'd had to jump off the chuck wagon and prod the mules into motion. Her head hurt from the glare of the sun.

But most of all her rear end hurt.

The wooden buckboard had turned harder and harder with each bump in the trail. Her blue jeans protected her from splinters, but she had more than one blister forming on her tender derriere. She suddenly wondered why greenhorns were referred to as tenderfoots. Tenderbutts would be more accurate.

Samson and Delilah balked again, bringing the chuck wagon to a halt. With a frustrated sigh, Calley leaped off the buckboard and strode up to the front of the mules. She stood between them, just far enough away to prevent Samson from treating her to another spray from his nose.

"All right, you two, we need to have a serious talk."

Samson and Delilah just looked at her.

"I know you're hot and tired," she said, wiping the perspiration off her brow. "So am I. But the sooner we get to the next campsite, the sooner we can all relax."

Delilah gave her a slow-eyed blink. Both mules had incredibly long eyelashes.

"If you don't give me any more trouble today, I

might even be able to find some more sugar cubes for you."

Delilah's ears perked up and she spread her lips back over her teeth.

"So do we have a deal?"

Samson snorted, spraying her dusty cowboy boots.

"I'll take that as a yes," Calley muttered, walking back to the chuck wagon. She grabbed the buckboard and hoisted herself up. Wincing slightly at the contact between her rear end and the rough wood, she picked up the harness reins.

Cliff Donovan rode up beside her. "Having problems?"

"Nothing I can't handle." She slapped the reins and the mules began trodding slowly forward.

"You really should have a hat on out here," Cliff said, his horse lumbering alongside the wagon. "The sun can be wicked, especially at this time of the day."

"I saw an old straw hat in the back of the wagon," she replied, satisfied that Samson and Delilah had finally decided to cooperate. She just hoped she had enough sugar cubes to last the rest of the cattle drive. "I'll put it on the next time we stop for water."

As soon as she said the word *water*, the mules came to an abrupt halt.

"Wonderful," she muttered, dropping the reins.

Cliff smiled. "I could let you in on Bud's secret."

She liked his smile. It reminded her of his daughter, Bianca. They shared the same red hair, too. "I'm ready to try anything."

He smiled down at the immobile mules. "This seems like valuable information under the circumstances. Is it worth a dried apple pie?"

"Definitely," she replied, certain she'd seen a recipe in the old trailhand's cookbook.

"Okay." Cliff leaned toward her. "He sings."

She blinked. "What?"

"The mules are used to Bud's singing. If he sings, they walk. When he stops, they stop."

She frowned. "But I can't carry a tune."

He shrugged. "Nobody will hear you out here except a bunch of steers and some bored cowboys."

She looked at Samson and Delilah. "Do they have any particular favorites?"

"Actually, I never paid that much attention." Cliff tipped up his cowboy hat. "But I'm partial to country-and-western songs. Especially Trisha Yearwood."

Calley sighed. "Sorry, that's not in my repertoire."

He shrugged. "I probably won't be in earshot anyway." He spurred his horse forward a few feet, then glanced back at her. "How soon can I have my pie?"

"Is tomorrow soon enough?"

"Yes, ma'am." Then he grinned, tipped his hat, and rode off toward the herd.

Calley stared at the recalcitrant mules. It was hard to believe two such obstinate animals had brought her to this point.

Then she opened her mouth and began to sing.

"WHAT THE HELL is that?" Matt asked, reining his horse to a stop. "Is one of the steers hurt?"

Cliff grinned. "I think it's Calley."

Matt winced as another high-pitched wail drifted toward him. "What's wrong with her?"

"Nothing. She's singing."

"Singing?" Matt sat motionless in the saddle,

straining to make out the words of a song. They carried over the herd in tuneless bits and snatches.

"'Oh, give me a home, where the buffalo roam...'"

"Well, I guess you could call it that," Cliff said, wincing a little. "I told her Bud used to sing to the mules."

Matt scowled. "I never heard Bud sing a song in my life."

"That may be true, but I figured we could use a little entertainment. And I finagled us a dried apple pie out of the deal, too."

Matt wheeled Jericho around and headed for the chuck wagon. This had to stop. First she'd wheedled her way onto the cattle drive and now this.

Calley smiled at him as he rode up, which caused an odd sensation in his chest. Probably indigestion from the onions she'd added to their breakfast this morning. And the way she was smiling, he feared he'd be eating a lot more of her breakfasts in the weeks to come.

Matt just didn't understand it. He'd expected this pretty city woman to turn tail and gallop back home before the first sundown. Instead, she'd not only taken on all of Bud's duties but actually seemed to be enjoying herself.

He'd spent the last two decades out on the range. It was a solitary life, with the occasional surly cowboy for company. That's the way he liked it. Now Calley Graham was turning his cattle drive upside down.

So why did he keep finding excuses to talk to her?

Because she was disrupting the drive, he told himself firmly. Distracting the cowboys from their work. And he couldn't afford to let that happen. Not with half a million dollars at stake.

"'Home, home on the range,'" she crooned, her voice cracking in the middle of the verse.

He winced, wondering why he was so damn intrigued by her. She wasn't beautiful, though he liked her silky blond hair and the way her blue eyes matched the wide-open sky. But he liked her smile best of all. It was like a ray of warm sunshine breaking through the clouds.

But that didn't mean she belonged here.

"Stop that," he called out to her, slowing his pace to match that of the mules.

"I can't stop now," she sang to the tune of the song.

Matt frowned. "You're spooking the cattle."

She laughed. "I noticed they've started moving a little faster. Do you suppose they're trying to get away from me?"

"I wouldn't be surprised," he replied, wishing he could get away from her himself. Wishing suddenly that he'd never met Calley Graham.

"Then that's a good thing, right? We'll just get to the Lazy R all the sooner."

That's what he wanted. To get to the Lazy R as soon as possible and get away from Calley. He opened his mouth, but she started singing again.

Matt gave up and spurred his horse back to the herd, her voice accompanying him all the way.

"Give the kid a break," Deb Gunn called to him from her horse. She was riding flank and had her hat pushed up high on her forehead, revealing a thick sprinkle of dark freckles. "She's having a great time."

Matt rode up behind a lagging steer and eased it back into the herd. "This isn't a vacation. This is work. I can't let her distract the crew."

Deb smiled. "She's not distracting me. But I'll find out if she's bothering the boys."

"That's not necessary," Matt began.

Deb ignored him, turning around in her saddle and calling out to her husband. "Is Calley distracting you, Davis?"

"Nope," Davis called back.

"How about you, Cliff?" Deb hollered to the lanky cowboy riding the west perimeter. "Is Calley bothering you?"

"Hell, no," Cliff shouted back. "I kinda like her singing. Gets damn boring out here without a radio."

"Ask Boyd if Calley is distracting him," Deb shouted.

Matt's jaw tightened as he watched Cliff gallop to the front of the herd. A few moments later he rode back to his position.

"Boyd says he likes her kind of distraction," Cliff shouted.

Deb cupped her hands around her mouth. "Arnie!"

The old cowboy didn't look up, just kept his gaze roaming over the cattle. She called to him again, louder this time, with the same result.

Then she turned back to Matt. "Arnie's hearing is bad, so I don't think Calley's distracting him, either." Her smile widened into a grin. "I think it just must be you, boss."

"Thanks for taking the survey," he muttered, riding back into his position on the outer flank. Then he heard Calley belt out the words to "You Are My Sunshine." And before he knew it, he was humming along.

CHAPTER EIGHT

BILL SIMMS stood on the front stoop of Liv Graham's bungalow in the suburbs of San Antonio and ran one hand over his hair. The musky scent of Old Spice was strong in his nostrils, making him worry that he'd overdone it with the cologne.

"Hell with it," he muttered, turning away from the house and back toward the street where his pickup truck was parked. Then he heard the door open behind him.

His palms began to sweat as he slowly turned around. Liv Graham stood in the doorway, looking every bit as beautiful as she had when he'd last seen her. Her ash-blond hair was loosely pulled back, her eyes just as blue. She had a few more lines on her face, but who the hell didn't?

Bill cleared his throat, then walked back to the porch. "Hello, Liv. I don't suppose you remember me?"

She smiled and held out one slender hand. "Bill Simms. My, it's been a long time."

"You still look wonderful."

"And you're still a charmer."

He could feel the heat creep up his neck. He'd been in a rocky marriage ten years ago and could still remember the sharp pang of envy he'd felt for Walt

Graham. How the man could have let a woman like Liv go was beyond his comprehension.

"I'm sorry about you and Walt," Bill began, then wanted to kick himself. What if she wasn't over the guy? "I stopped by the station the other day to visit a few of the old-timers who are still around. They mentioned you two split up a few years ago."

She nodded, but didn't seem distraught. "We grew apart. It happens sometimes."

A fact for which Bill found himself surprisingly grateful.

She waved him inside. "Please come in, Bill. I think I have Walt's address around here somewhere."

Bill followed her into the house, relishing the cool air that greeted him. He was dripping with perspiration. A reaction he couldn't blame on the mildly warm afternoon.

Liv led him into an airy living room, the southwestern decor simple but comfortable. Pale-turquoise pillows dotted the cream-colored sofa and small scattered seashells adorned a glass-topped coffee table. "I just made some fresh lemonade. Can I talk you into a glass?"

"That sounds mighty fine," he replied, seating himself in one of the armchairs. While she headed for the kitchen, he looked around the room. Framed photographs graced all the walls.

And Calley was in every one.

"Here we go," Liv said, returning to the living room with two frosty glasses of lemonade in her hands. She handed one to him, then seated herself on the sofa. He took the armchair opposite her.

Liv took a sip of lemonade. "I know I've got

Walt's new address around here somewhere, but do you think I can find it?''

''I'm not here for Walt's address,'' Bill told her, realizing he should have made the reason for his visit clear from the beginning. Although he wasn't entirely sure it was the real reason.

''Oh?''

He cleared his throat. ''When I stopped by the police station, one of the boys mentioned that you'd filed a missing person report on your daughter.''

Her eyes widened. ''Have they heard something? Have they found Calley?''

''I saw her just a week ago, Liv.''

She blinked. ''Where?''

''In New Mexico.''

She set down her lemonade on the coffee table and he could see her fingers shaking. ''Where in New Mexico? And what was she doing there? If she has any idea how frantic I've been—''

''She's fine, Liv,'' he assured her. ''She was working on behalf of a detective agency, same as me. We were both on the trail of a cowboy named Matt Radcliffe. And we both found him right about the same time, on the open range just outside of Fort Sumner.''

She took a moment to digest his words. ''So if she found this man, why hasn't she come home?''

Bill shrugged. ''When we caught up with him, he was embarking on a cattle drive. The guy's a beneficiary in a will, but he refused to come back to Texas to collect his inheritance. Maybe she's still tryin' to change his mind. Or waiting around until the cattle drive ends. Radcliffe made it clear he wasn't interested, though.''

A smile haunted Liv's lips. "My daughter can be awfully stubborn when she puts her mind to it."

"I just wanted to let you know she's okay. So you don't have to worry."

"A mother always worries." She reached for her lemonade, her hand steadier now. "I think it's one of the requirements of the job."

He chuckled. "Hey, I've got three grown daughters myself. That's one of the reasons I don't have as much hair as I used to."

Her gaze flickered up to his thinning gray hair and Bill wanted to kick himself again. The last thing he needed to do was call attention to his flaws. Hell, he was probably wasting his time here anyway. A woman like Liv Graham would never look twice at an old retired cop like him.

He drained his glass, then stood up. "Thank you for the lemonade."

Liv followed him to the door. "It was wonderful to see you again, Bill. And I can't thank you enough for telling me about Calley."

He turned at the door. "Your daughter sure looked better than the last time I saw her. Fact is, I didn't even recognize her till I heard her name. Guess it's true that medical science really can work miracles."

Liv's lower lip quivered until she pressed her mouth tightly together. Then she took a deep breath. "Calley's not as healthy as she appears. That's why I've been so worried about her. She may seem fine, but that could change at any moment. That's what happened when she first got sick. She was fine one moment, then in critical condition the next."

Bill shifted on his feet, wishing he knew a way to reassure her. "I didn't realize she was still sick."

Liv gave a shaky nod. "Calley likes to pretend she's fine, but the truth is that her heart could give out at any time. That's why I've had to watch her so closely all these years. Make sure she didn't overexert herself or take any unnecessary risks."

He looked into her blue eyes. "You're an incredible woman, Liv."

She met his gaze, a pink blush staining her cheeks. "Thank you, Bill. And thank you again for coming here today and telling me about Calley. It's a relief just to know where she is. Or at least where she was a week ago. Naturally, I've been thinking the worst."

He hesitated, wondering if he should take a chance. His concern for her overcame his own insecurities. "I think you need a break, Liv. Why don't you join me for dinner tonight? There's a new Italian restaurant on the River Walk. We could catch up after all these years."

She smiled, then shook her head. "I'm sorry, Bill. I can't risk it. Calley might call. She might need me."

He nodded, trying hard to hide his disappointment. "Sure, I understand. Just thought it was worth a shot." He hesitated. "If you ever change your mind and get a craving for pasta, give me a call. I'm in the phone book."

"Thanks, Bill," she replied, not making any promises.

He could see in her eyes that she wasn't going to be dialing his number anytime soon.

"Right now," she continued, "the only thing I can think about is getting Calley home safe and sound."

CALLEY DISHED UP a bowl of Son-of-a-Gun Stew. "Where's Matt?"

Deb sighed as she reached for a slightly scorched biscuit. "Somehow we lost three steers on the trail today. Matt is backtracking to see if he can round them up."

"But they were all here this morning." Calley remembered Matt taking the time to count them before they started on the trail. Just like they'd done every morning for the past week.

Deb shrugged as she took the full bowl from Calley. "I figure we lost them when we made that river crossing."

Calley had been too concerned with keeping the chuck wagon upright in the water to keep an eye on the cattle. It had been both terrifying and exhilarating.

"You think they might have drowned?"

"Strayed off is more like it. Walking neck-deep in water isn't high on the list of fun times for most critters. I'm just surprised one of us didn't notice."

Calley stirred the stew left in the bottom of the pot. "Do you expect him back soon?"

"Hard to say. We really can't afford to lose those three steers. Three more and this drive is over."

"What do you mean?"

"It's all part of that bet Tupper made. Matt's got to bring in ninety-five percent of the herd to the Lazy R. Otherwise, we lose." Deb shook her head as she added another biscuit to her plate. "Davis and I are counting on the wages from this drive to start building a dude ranch on my land in Wyoming."

Matt had told Calley about the bet, but hadn't mentioned the finer details. She replaced the lid on the pot as Deb walked over to join the rest of the crew. The sooner this cattle drive ended, the sooner she could take Matt back to Finders Keepers. And find a pharmacy to refill her prescription. She only had three pills left.

But part of her didn't want the drive to end. Not if it meant Matt would lose the bet. And Davis and Deb would lose the money they needed for their dude ranch. She thought about the Donovans and little Bianca. Katie Donovan had made it clear how important this job was to their family. And old Arnie seemed thrilled just to be needed.

It seemed the only one who wouldn't be disappointed if the cattle drive ended was Boyd. Although in the last week she'd already seen a slight change in him. He was too busy and too tired most of the time to brag about his riches or his sexual prowess. A welcome change for everyone on the drive.

Several hours later, Calley awoke at the sound of tin clinking against tin. She glanced at the alarm clock and saw that it was just after midnight. Rising from the bedroll, she tucked her shirt into her jeans, then quickly finger combed her hair before climbing out the back of the wagon.

Matt stood silhouetted by the fire, a cup of steaming coffee in his hand.

"Did you find the missing steers?" Calley asked softly.

He looked up at her, the light from the full moon illuminating the stubble on his jaw. "You should be in bed."

She smiled. "Is that a yes or a no?"

"Yes." He turned back to the fire.

"Well, that's a relief."

She retrieved a bowl from the back of the chuck wagon, then walked over to the fire. She'd left the pot hanging high above the flames to keep the stew warm. Reaching for the ladle, she spooned up a generous portion, then handed it to him. "I saved you some supper."

"Thanks." He took the bowl, then seated himself on one of the upturned crates the crew used for chairs. "I'm starving."

He wore a shearling jacket and well-worn jeans, along with the familiar black Stetson. She sat opposite him, watching him eat in silence. His hands dwarfed the bowl and spoon. She found herself wondering how it would feel to be touched by those hands. To have her bare skin stroked by those long fingers. To run her own hands over his solid chest and wide shoulders. To feel the rough scrape of his whiskers on her cheek.

"Calley?"

She blinked, then realized he was staring at her. No doubt because she'd been staring at him. Blood rushed into her cheeks, just as it had warmed other parts of her body while she'd been lost in her fantasy.

"Yes?"

"Thanks for the stew." He set the empty bowl on the ground beside him. "It was great."

She laughed. "An empty stomach always helps it taste better."

His mouth turned up in a half smile. "Maybe so."

"You have to admit my cooking is getting better every day."

His smile widened. "Only if you admit you lied to get this job."

"*Lied* is a strong word. I prefer the term *creative exaggeration.*"

"You can say that again." He shook his head, a low chuckle carrying through the night air. "I've sure never tasted anything like Calley's Special Trail Wraps before. And I hope I never do again.''

''Actually, we're having them for supper tomorrow night,'' she teased.

''Can we have antacid pie for dessert?''

''Very funny, cowboy.'' The cool night air made her shiver. She stood up and moved closer to the fire.

''Here,'' Matt said, removing his jacket.

''No, I'm fine,'' she protested.

But he draped it over her shoulders anyway. It had absorbed the warmth from his body, sending a delicious tingle through her. She pulled the jacket closer around her. ''Thank you.''

Matt poured himself another cup of coffee, then sat back down. ''You should probably be in bed. We have another long day ahead of us tomorrow.''

''I'm a big girl. I can stay up all night if I want to.''

He looked at her over the rim of his cup, the expression in his eyes sending another tingle through her. He looked hungry. And not for stew.

She swallowed hard, wondering if it was wishful thinking or perhaps her lack of experience with men that made her so aware of his every movement. She found herself oddly fascinated with his hands. His smile. The low rumble of his voice.

''That's what I plan to do,'' he said at last.

''What?'' Calley realized she'd lost track of the conversation.

''I'm going to stay up all night.''

''Why? You already found the missing steers.''

''That's right.'' His jaw tightened. ''I found all three of them dead in a ravine with their throats slit.''

Icy dread filled her veins. "Who would do such a thing?"

"That's what I intend to find out—before it happens again. Someone is trying to sabotage this cattle drive. And I'm starting to believe it might be someone on this crew."

"No." Calley couldn't accept that possibility. Not when she'd spent more than a week with these people. Shared meals and jokes. Heard their hopes and dreams. "Couldn't it be someone from Hobbs's crew? That makes more sense, doesn't it? I mean, it couldn't be one of us."

He took another sip of his coffee, then tossed the rest into the fire. The flames popped and sizzled. "I don't want to believe it either, Calley. I have no doubt Hobbs is behind it. But I sure as hell don't see how he could do this kind of damage without help from the inside."

"Who?"

He shrugged. "That's the hell of it. I don't have any proof. Except I know that broken axle on the chuck wagon was no accident. Or those dead steers. And then there are the holes."

Her brow furrowed. "Holes?"

"I scouted out the trail ahead early this morning and found several freshly dug holes. Just big enough for a steer or a horse to step in and break its leg."

"You think someone dug those holes deliberately?"

He nodded. "That's why we made the river crossing today. It lengthened the route a little, but may have saved us a few head in the long run."

"So that's why Boyd was grumbling so much about crossing the river."

"It wasn't part of the planned route. And it not only cost us time, but made both the cowboys and horses work harder. Something I can't allow to go on if we want to beat Hobbs to the Lazy R."

"Does the rest of the crew know the reason?"

He shook his head. "I'm the one in charge of this drive, so it's my responsibility. Besides, the worst thing that could happen to this crew is to start casting blame on one another."

Calley couldn't argue with that. She enjoyed the easy camaraderie of the crew. It had given her something she hadn't enjoyed in a very long time—friends. "So what are you going to do?"

"Catch the culprit," he said simply.

"But how?"

"By keeping a better eye out during the day for anything unusual. And by taking over the night shift from now on."

She smiled. "You think you can stay awake for twenty-four hours a day?"

He shrugged. "I'll do what I have to do."

"Let me help."

He looked at her. "Why?"

Because I want to do something important for once in my life. Because it might make you smile. Because you matter to me. But Calley didn't give him any of those reasons. "I already get up at four o'clock to start breakfast. I can wake up an hour early and watch for anything suspicious. That way you can get at least a few hours of sleep."

Then another thought occurred to her. "Unless you suspect me."

He smiled. "Be kind of dumb of me to confide in you if I thought you were behind all this."

"So you trust me?"

"I guess I do," he replied, looking just as surprised by that admission.

She felt a ridiculous surge of pleasure rise up inside of her.

"Besides, it would be almost impossible for you to cut three steers from the herd while driving the chuck wagon."

"So how do you think it happened?"

"When some of the cattle lag behind or wander off, one of us always goes after them. It would be easy enough to ride off after ten strays and only bring back seven without anyone noticing. Especially during the chaos of a river crossing."

"So do you have any hunches about who's responsible?"

"I'd rather not say until I know for certain."

She respected his silence. Accusing the wrong person could only lead to hard feelings, although she guessed the most likely suspect was obvious to both of them. Boyd Tupper was the only cowboy who wouldn't be disappointed if the cattle drive was cut short. But she hated to think that Boyd was capable of that kind of betrayal.

She stood up. "I think I'll go back to bed now. But I'll set my alarm for three o'clock and take over the watch."

He rose to his feet and stepped closer to her. "Are you sure?"

She shrugged off his jacket and held it out to him. "I really do want to help."

He reached for his jacket, his hand closing around hers. "Thank you."

She swallowed at the sensation, then glanced up at

his face. His eyes were very dark and the way he was looking at her made her blood swirl low in her belly.

He leaned closer for one brief moment, then pulled back, taking both his hand and the jacket away from her. "I owe you."

Calley watched him walk away, shocked by her unexpected reaction to his words. She didn't want Matt Radcliffe to owe her.

She wanted him to kiss her.

CHAPTER NINE

MATT SETTLED into a routine during the next week. He'd lead the cattle drive during the day, then nap while the rest of the crew ate supper and swapped stories over the campfire. After they retired for the night, Calley would wake him with a smile and a warmed-up supper plate. Then she'd disappear inside the chuck wagon to sleep until the alarm roused her again at three in the morning.

At first, he'd barely been able to keep his eyes open during the day, almost falling out of his saddle more than once. The crew had accepted the new shift schedule with only a few raised eyebrows. Davis had asked outright why Matt had volunteered to work every night. But a sharp elbow in the ribs from Deb, followed by a nod in Calley's direction, had silenced him. Matt knew they all believed he just wanted to spend time alone with her.

And he let them believe it.

"You should get some sleep," Calley said early one morning as she combed her shimmering hair in front of the fire. He'd accidentally come upon her the day before while she was bathing in the river, though she hadn't seen him.

He'd seen just enough of her to leave him wanting more. Her creamy bare shoulders had risen just far enough above the water to tell him she wasn't wearing anything underneath. He hadn't stayed to find out, although he'd been damn tempted.

"I'm fine," he lied, not wanting to mention the effect she was having on his body. "But you look like you could use a cup of coffee."

"I've never been a coffee drinker," she said, looking longingly at his steaming cup.

"How come?"

"My mother always told me caffeine was bad for me." She closed her eyes and inhaled deeply. "But it smells wonderful."

He handed over his cup. "Go ahead, Calley. Live dangerously."

A spark of amusement lit her eyes. "You're right. That is my motto." She took the cup from him, then hesitated. "Do you recommend cream or sugar?"

"No, ma'am. Black and strong is the only way to go. And this batch is strong enough to grow hair on your chest."

She laughed. "I'm not sure I want to live *that* dangerously."

He wondered if she realized how appealing she looked in the firelight. The way her skin glowed and her blue eyes sparkled. She wore an oversize flannel shirt to ward off the early-morning chill and a faded pair of denim jeans. They hugged her hips and sheathed a pair of long, slender legs.

He suddenly wished he had something stronger than coffee to help take his mind off Calley. Although, if he was honest with himself, it was more than her physical attributes that had captured his attention. He found himself looking forward to their predawn chats over the campfire. Matt's weariness seemed to vanish as soon as Calley emerged from the chuck wagon. She had an energy about her, a sunny idealism that drove the shadows of his past away.

"Ready or not," she said, holding up the coffee cup, "here I go." Then she took a cautious sip of the steaming brew.

"Well?" he asked.

She grimaced. "It's not too bad."

He laughed at her pained expression. "Liar."

"Okay, it's awful." She handed the cup back to him. "I guess I haven't been missing anything. At least where coffee is concerned."

He reached for the coffeepot and topped off his cup. "I suppose it's an acquired taste. Like chewing tobacco."

Her eyes widened. "Do you have some?"

"Don't tell me you want to try that, too?"

She shrugged. "Why not? I'm ready and willing to live dangerously."

"There's living dangerously, and then there's living stupid. Haven't you heard that chewing tobacco causes cancer?"

She nodded. "True. And I think there's spitting involved, too. Maybe I'll pass on the chewing tobacco."

"I'm glad to see you've got some sense."

She batted her eyelashes at him and spoke in a flirtatious southern drawl. "Why, Mr. Radcliffe, you sure know how to turn a gal's head with all that flatterin' talk."

He grinned in spite of himself. "Aren't you supposed to be making breakfast?"

"Aren't you supposed to be catching a few winks before the sun comes up?"

He took another sip of his coffee. "I've decided to

alter the plan a bit, since nothing suspicious has happened in almost a week.''

"But that's a good thing, isn't it?"

He shrugged. "Depends how you look at it. If there's a rattler waiting to strike, I'd rather know where he's at before he bites."

"So what's your new plan?"

His gaze dropped to the fire. "I'm going to lull the culprit into a sense of security. Make him think I've got my mind on other things."

"Like what?"

"Not what. Who." He looked up at her and cleared his throat. "You."

She stared at him.

Matt could feel the blush crawling up his neck and just hoped Calley couldn't see it in the firelight. "I figured if the traitor thought I was focusing all my attention on our pretty cook instead of the cattle drive, he might try to make another move."

She took a step away from the fire. "Why me?"

"Because I refuse to pretend I have a crush on Boyd, no matter how much money is at stake."

He wished he could see her face, but it was hidden in the shadows. Hell, he'd never meant to make her uncomfortable. Or worse, make her think he expected her to act out their faux romance.

"I just wanted you to know the reason why I'll be spending more time with you," he explained, hoping to reassure her. Wondering if it sounded as lame to her ears as it did to his own.

"Oh."

He dumped the rest of his coffee onto the ground. "Maybe it's a stupid idea."

She didn't say anything as he got up and rinsed his

cup in the bucket. He could hear the sound of a cough from the pup tent where the Gunns slept. The first rays of dawn now streaked across the sky and he could see Boyd sitting up in his bedroll, his hair spiked in every direction.

"Looks like we'll get an early start this morning." He turned toward his horse, but Calley stepped in his path.

She glanced over her shoulder at Boyd, then looked up at Matt again. "It's not a stupid idea." She moved closer to him. "Especially for two people who like to live dangerously."

Then she kissed him.

Matt was completely unprepared for the touch of her soft lips on his mouth. Tender. Tentative. Then she circled her arms around his neck and leaned into him.

He didn't need any further encouragement. He wrapped his arms around her waist and pulled her closer, reveling in the taste of her and the alluring scent of her skin. Her luscious curves fit perfectly against his hard body and he captured her sigh as his tongue breached the seam of her lips.

Her fingers trailed through his hair, dislodging his cowboy hat and causing it to fall to the ground behind him.

Desire, hot and fierce, poured through his veins, pooling low in his groin. Reminding him that he hadn't held a woman in a very long time. Especially a woman as enticing as Calley. She felt so good in his arms. So right. He heard himself groan as her tongue delicately explored his mouth. Teasing and tantalizing until he wanted to do more than kiss her.

So much more.

Matt pulled back, breaking the kiss before he lost what little control he had left. Calley stared up at him, her blue eyes wide and her lips full and red.

"Wow," she said at last.

He took a deep gulp of air, all too aware that Calley wasn't the only one staring at him. Boyd was now on his feet, his hands on his hips and a disgruntled expression on his face. The Gunns had emerged from their tent and were standing by Cliff, all three of them grinning.

"Why did you do that?" Matt asked in a low voice, sounding more gruff than he'd intended.

"It was your idea," she said softly, her fingers rubbing her cheek.

He could see redness there and knew his beard stubble had made the mark. "Damn it, Calley. All I had in mind was talking."

She tilted her head as she looked at him, confusion clouding her blue eyes. "Was it so awful?"

Awful? Was she serious? "No. It was just... unexpected." He raked one hand through his hair, wondering how he could explain it to her when even he didn't understand the riot of emotions churning through him.

"I'm sorry if I offended you," she said, not looking the least bit sorry to him. "I thought I was helping put your new plan into action." She glanced over at the crew, who were now pretending not to watch the show. "At least they think something's going on. That's a start, isn't it?"

"Can you at least give me a little warning next time?"

"Don't worry, Matt," she said, turning toward

the chuck wagon. "There won't be a next time."

He watched her disappear inside the wagon, then heard the loud clank of pots and pans.

Cliff walked up beside him. "Now that's the sound of an angry woman."

"I'm not exactly sure what just happened here," Matt mused. "I think I must have said the wrong thing."

"I'd say there's no doubt about it." Cliff clapped him on the back, then headed toward his horse.

A thud sounded in the chuck wagon, followed by a muffled oath. Matt smiled. He might have been wrong, but so was she. There would definitely be a next time.

CALLEY SAT on a wooden trunk in the chuck wagon, cradling her sore toe. She'd dropped an industrial-size can of stewed tomatoes on it, then made matters worse by hitting her head on another ham.

It was all Matt's fault. That big, dumb, irresistible cowboy had completely befuddled her. She'd thought one kiss would be harmless fun.

She'd never been so wrong.

Kissing Matt Radcliffe had been one of the most exciting, wonderful, terrifying experiences of her life. She'd expected to like it. She hadn't expected it to completely shatter her self-control.

Calley took a deep breath, remembering the way her knees had shaken. The way Matt's body had felt against hers. The way his tongue had swept into her mouth, sparking that mindless desire. She closed her eyes, her cheek still burning slightly from the way his whiskers had grazed her skin.

For so many years she'd wondered how it would feel to kiss a man. But she'd never imagined him tasting like leather and wood smoke. Holding her like he never wanted to let her go. Kissing her until she could barely stand.

But he'd obviously had the opposite reaction. Her cheeks burned when she remembered the shocked expression on his face. She'd read in *Cosmo* magazine that men liked it when the woman made the first move. Obviously, *Cosmo* hadn't interviewed any cowboys lately.

"Knock, knock."

Calley looked up to see Deb Gunn standing at the back of the wagon.

"May I come in?"

"Sure," Calley said, although the last thing she wanted was company.

Deb hitched her leg over the back end of the wagon and climbed in. "I see you've taken my advice and decided to use a little sugar on Matt."

Calley sighed. "I'm starting to think a good kick in the butt might have been the better choice."

Deb's brow furrowed. "Why? Looks to me like you could lead that man anywhere."

"Then you must not have seen the look on his face after I kissed him. I don't have a lot of experience with men," she admitted. "I probably did it wrong."

Deb laughed. "Then heaven help that man if you ever get it right. He could barely walk in a straight line after that kiss."

"I think you're just trying to make me feel better."

"Is it working?"

She smiled. "Yes."

"Good. But I meant every word I said. Davis had

that same stupefied expression on his face the first time we kissed. 'Course, he'd just been bucked off a horse and was still lying on the ground when I planted one on him.''

"I think this is different," Calley said, more confused than ever.

"Maybe so," Deb agreed. "But there's one thing that's as clear as the big blue sky. Matt Radcliffe is all yours. If you want him."

CHAPTER TEN

THE NEXT DAY, Calley was even more confused by Matt's behavior. He'd barely said a word at breakfast, then seemed to be avoiding her the rest of the day. Yet she'd caught him staring at her more than once. For her part, she kept replaying that kiss over and over in her mind.

And she didn't regret it one bit.

But now that night had fallen, her self-assurance began to wane. The rest of the crew had gone to bed over an hour ago, but she'd put off waking Matt. Partly because she knew he was exhausted. And partly because she was jittery about spending time alone with him again.

Realizing she couldn't avoid it any longer, she walked over to his bedroll and gently shook his shoulder. Matt's eyes opened and he looked up at her.

"Time to rise and shine," she said softly, resisting the urge to trace her fingers over the shadow of beard stubbling her face.

He sat up, still fully clothed, then reached for his boots. "What time is it?"

"A little after midnight."

"You should be in bed."

"Not if we're sticking to our plan."

He rose to his feet, his dark eyes unfathomable in the moonlight. "What did you have in mind?"

Calley itched to kiss him again, just to throw him off-balance. And to satisfy her own curiosity. Had that first kiss been a fluke of nature? Or would her entire world ignite again if their lips touched?

"I thought we could talk for a while," she replied, turning toward the campfire. "I kept your supper warm and made a fresh pot of coffee."

He rubbed one hand over his jaw, not saying anything for a moment. Then he gave a sharp nod. "I'll be there in a few minutes."

She walked to the chuck wagon, trying to ignore the ridiculous fluttering in the pit of her stomach. She'd spent time alone with Matt before. This night was no different.

Only it was different.

Everything had changed when she kissed him. She could feel it in the way he looked at her. There was a tension between them—thick and electric. Now she just had to decide if that was good or bad.

When Matt finally appeared at the campfire, it was obvious he'd been down to the river. His dark hair was wet under his cowboy hat and his cheeks freshly shaven.

"Hope you're hungry," she said, handing him a plate.

"Starved." He picked up his fork and began eating as she took a seat on the crate next to him.

Neither of them said anything while he ate. Calley listened to the crackle of the fire and the plaintive howls of a pack of coyotes. A full moon shone in the night sky, illuminating everything in its ethereal glow. Despite having spent two weeks on the range, she was still in awe of the stark beauty surrounding her.

"Thank you, Calley."

She turned to look at him. "For what?"

"The coffee. The food." He set his empty plate down beside him. "Keeping me company."

She smiled. "My pleasure."

He looked up at the night sky. "Have you made a wish?"

She followed his gaze, noticing for the first time the lone star twinkling above her. "Star light, star bright," she breathed, reciting the old nursery rhyme. "First star I see tonight. I wish I may, I wish I might, have the wish I wish tonight."

Then she closed her eyes and made her wish.

"Well?" Matt's voice was low and husky. "What did you wish for?"

She opened her eyes. "I wished that no one on this cattle drive is guilty of sabotage. That whoever is responsible for breaking Bud's arm and killing those steers and digging those holes just finally gave up and went away."

"That's a pretty unselfish wish. Don't you want anything for yourself?"

She didn't tell him that she'd been making a selfish wish on the stars for the last ten years. A wish for a normal life. A wish that had never come true. Funny how tonight's wish, which would help not only herself, but Matt and the Gunns and Cliff if it came true, made her feel so good inside.

She gazed up at the star. "Everybody wins something if this cattle drive is successful. You'll be able to buy your ranch. Deb and Davis can build a home and business on her land in Wyoming. Cliff can go back to Santa Fe instead of looking for cowboy work that separates him from his family. And I can take you back to Finders Keepers with me and hire on permanently. That's what I want most.''

He stared at her. ''Is it, Calley?''

Her mouth grew dry as she looked into his eyes. Raw desire sparked in those dark, stormy depths. She gave a shaky nod, not trusting herself to speak. Then she took a deep breath, trying to regain her equilibrium. ''What about you? What did you wish for, Matt?''

He turned his gaze up to the sky. ''The same wish I've made since I was twelve years old. A ranch to call my own.''

''In New Mexico?''

He smiled. ''I can't imagine settling down anywhere but Texas. That's where I grew up. It's always seemed like home to me.''

''Won't you miss nights like this out on the range?''

He shook his head. ''I've lived the wandering life for almost twenty years, Calley. Worked for some of the biggest ranches in the West. But I've always wanted something more....''

His voice trailed off, but she didn't say anything, sensing that Matt didn't open up like this to everyone. Maybe it was the serenity of the night. Or the full moon, casting an unearthly glow on everything it touched.

Her tension eased, though her heart still skittered in her chest. She hoped the staccato rhythm was caused by Matt's nearness and not because she'd run out of her heart medicine three days ago. She'd had no unusual signs or symptoms. No reason to fear her health might be in danger.

In fact, Matt Radcliffe might pose the most dangerous risk to her heart yet. Especially if he kept looking at her that way.

"I want a home," he said at last. "Somewhere that belongs to me. Somewhere that I belong. It doesn't have to be big. Or beautiful. Or make me rich. It just has to be mine."

She could hear the longing in his voice. "Don't you have anywhere to call a home?"

He tossed the rest of his coffee on the ground. "No."

Just like that, the intimacy between them vanished. She could tell by the shuttered expression on his face that he was through talking. At least Calley finally understood why the success of this drive was so important to him. Matt Radcliffe wanted more than the money. He was chasing a dream.

She cupped her chin in her hand, realizing that they were both chasing a dream. Matt wanted to find a home of his own, and she wanted to escape a home that had become her prison. She steeled herself against the guilt that wanted to niggle its way into her heart. She loved her mother, but she couldn't live with her anymore. Life with Liv Graham didn't count as a life at all. Not when Liv was in a constant state of fear and worry. It had driven Calley's father away. And it had finally driven Calley away, too.

Running out of her heart medication had scared Calley at first. But there was no going back now. She had decided to live her life dangerously. And that danger included Matt Radcliffe. Her eyelids grew heavy as she stared up at the sky. If the cattle drive proceeded on schedule, they'd be due to arrive at the Lazy R in Jacksboro in about a fortnight. Then she could refill her prescription, as well as accomplish what she'd set out to do—bring Matt Radcliffe back to Finders Keepers.

After that... Calley wouldn't let herself think that far ahead. She'd learned a long time ago to cherish each day and not worry about the future. She closed her eyes, her head nodding forward. Then she started when she realized someone was lifting her off the crate.

"Relax," Matt murmured as he carried her in his arms. "I've got you."

He held her cradled against his chest and she could feel the strong, steady beat of his heart. He walked over to the chuck wagon and set her gently inside. "Sweet dreams, Calley."

She reached up to trace his jaw with her fingertips. "Good night, Matt."

He hesitated for a moment, then turned on his heel and walked away.

Calley felt a little dizzy, but she blamed it on her exhaustion and the heady sensation of being carried in Matt's arms.

If only he knew how much she'd wanted to stay there.

MATT REFUSED to take another plunge into the Brazos River. He'd done it once already tonight, right after Calley had roused him from an erotic dream. About her.

Now he sat on his horse, staring into the water. His midnight skinny-dip hadn't cooled his desire for her. If anything, it was stronger than ever.

He wheeled Jericho away from the river, then began to slowly circle the perimeter of the quiet herd.

The lone wishing star had now disappeared among the twinkling canopy above him.

He heard a rustle in the brush ahead, followed by the squawk of panicked prairie chickens. No doubt a coyote had found their roosting place and decided to stay for supper. While the world slept, the night came alive out on the range. Nocturnal hunters like owls and hawks traversed the sky. Coyotes, possums, raccoons and all kinds of four-legged varmints roamed the land.

And it looked as if a two-legged varmint had preyed on Cliff's horse.

Matt swore under his breath when he saw the palomino mare favoring a hind leg. Climbing off his saddle, Matt secured Jericho's reins to the low-hanging tree branch, then approached Cliff's horse.

It snorted and sidestepped as Matt drew nearer, pain and fear making the mare skittish. He murmured soothing words, slowing his approach. Then he reached out one hand and smoothed it tenderly over the horse's neck. At last she began to calm, allowing him to move closer to the hind leg so he could inspect the damage.

Gently manipulating the fetlock with his fingers, he didn't feel any swelling or noticeable injury. Yet the horse was obviously in pain.

Then he saw it.

A rusty razor blade had been wedged into the back of the hoof, too high up for the mare to have picked it up accidentally. With each step the mare had taken, the razor blade had sliced a little bit farther into the coronet band, right below the fetlock, until at last it became too sore for the palomino to stand on.

Blood and pus oozed on his fingertips as he carefully prodded the open wound. He wiped his hand on his jeans, then tried to pull the razor blade out.

"Damn," he muttered, slicing his thumb on the corner of the blade. It was stuck tight.

He reached for the pliers he kept in a leather holster on his belt, then tugged on the razor blade, finally pulling it free. Matt had brought some antibiotic ointment he could use to treat the wound, but it was obvious that Cliff's horse would be too lame to handle a rider for the rest of the journey.

He stood up, rubbing one hand over his jaw. Despite the evidence, he didn't want to believe any of his crew could be capable of such violence toward an animal. The slit throats of those three steers had been bad enough. But to do this kind of damage to a horse was a form of slow torture.

Who the hell would want to stop the cattle drive badly enough to resort to this kind of cruelty?

He thought about Marla's curse as he unhitched Jericho's reins from the tree branch. Then he climbed into the saddle and headed back toward the camp. He'd wanted to draw the culprit out by pretending he was too absorbed with Calley to notice anything else.

Only his plan had backfired on him.

Calley had been on his mind ever since that kiss. Hell, he was so absorbed with her tonight, he probably would have missed a stampede. That had to change.

It was time to catch the sadistic thief who wanted to steal his dream.

CHAPTER ELEVEN

THE NEXT MORNING, Calley walked down to a narrow fork of the Brazos river, the light from the moon illuminating her path. She liked this time of day best, before the sun rose to wake both the cattle and the cowboys.

She knelt down at the bank of the river, scooping up a bucket of clear, cold water. Then she filled the other bucket and set it beside her. With a deep sigh, she looked out over the water. A bird sat on top of a rock in the middle of the stream, stretching its wings. On the opposite bank, she glimpsed a doe emerging from the shadows with a young fawn by her side.

The doe was tense and alert as she approached the water's edge, hypersensitive to any potential danger to her babe. Watching the pair, Calley was swept back into memories of her own mother. Liv Graham had refused to allow any harm, real or imagined, to come to her daughter. Only Liv's natural instinct to protect had metamorphosed into an unhealthy obsession. By trying to *protect* her daughter, she had harmed Calley in more ways than she could ever imagine.

It had driven Calley's father away, and her friends as well. And any chance Calley had for romance. She closed her eyes, remembering the first man who had asked her out on a date.

Brian Haynes. They had met in the parking lot of

the medical complex where she went for her check-ups. A college student, Brian drove a taxi part-time to pay his way through school. He'd driven her home that day, one of the rare times her mother had been unable to chauffeur her.

Somewhere between the doctor's office and Calley's house, Brian had shyly asked Calley if she was dating anyone.

The answer was no. *Never.* But that was a fact she'd been too embarrassed to admit, since she was twenty years old at the time.

When he asked her for a date, she didn't hesitate. It was a rebellious step toward independence from her mother. One that had made her giddy, excited and happier than she could remember.

Only her joy hadn't lasted long.

Their date had been tense and awkward. The flirtatious Brian had disappeared, replaced by a man who kept taking surreptitious glances at his watch. And their good-night kiss, the one Calley had anticipated from the moment he'd asked her out, never came.

That's when she found out that Liv had gotten to him.

Her mother had told Brian all about Calley's heart condition when he'd come to pick her up for their date. While Calley had been nervously making last-minute touches to her hair and choosing just the right lipstick, Liv had told Brian how unwise it was for her daughter to be dating at all. Told him that any excitement could be extremely dangerous. That Calley could never risk having children. And though she might look healthy now, her condition could change in an instant, as it had before.

The poor man had been terrified. And no wonder.

Liv had painted him a picture of a woman who could literally die in his arms.

After that first awkward date, she never saw or heard from him again.

Calley opened her eyes, the ache of the past reverberating deep inside of her. The doe and fawn had disappeared. She pushed back thoughts of her mother, refusing to let the past cloud the present.

"Let me have this," she whispered to the wind and the water. "I just want to know how it feels to live like a normal person. To work. To laugh." She thought about Matt Radcliffe and that wondrous kiss they'd shared. Her first kiss. "To love."

The low of a steer in the distance reminded Calley that she didn't have time to sit around daydreaming. The crew would be up in another hour and ready for breakfast. She rose to her feet, grabbed both buckets by the handle, then turned around.

And ran right into Matt.

He reached out to catch her as she stumbled backward, water sloshing out of both buckets.

She regained her balance, her pulse racing. "Don't you know it's impolite to sneak up on a person like that?"

"Sorry." He reached up to brush a stray tendril of hair out of her eyes. "I didn't mean to scare you."

A blush warmed her cheeks. "How long have you been standing there?"

"Long enough to hear you talking to yourself." He smiled. "But don't worry. I couldn't hear what you were saying."

Relief washed over her. "Really?"

"Not a word." He glanced over his shoulder at the

still-peaceful camp. "Listen, we don't have much time."

She set down the buckets. "Time for what?"

"I want to set a trap." Matt took a step closer to her. "And I want you to be the bait."

NEITHER MATT NOR Calley said a word as they rode Jericho slowly up a small outcropping of rocks north of the campsite. Her slender arms were wrapped around his waist and her body pressed against his back, warming him in more ways than one.

"Do you really think this is going to work?" Her breath curled in his ear, causing Matt to sternly admonish himself to keep his mind on his plan.

"It's a long shot," he admitted as he spurred Jericho up a steep ascent.

Her arms tightened around his middle. "And all you want me to do is wait here?"

"Wait and watch. I'll wake the crew and tell them you're missing. We'll start a search, which will leave the camp unattended. That will be a perfect opportunity for anyone who wants to cause mischief."

She considered his words for a moment. "And if I don't see anything suspicious?"

"Then I'm putting an end to this cattle drive." They reached a plateau and he reined in his horse. "This looks like the right place. You'll have a good view of the campsite without anyone spotting you."

Swinging his left leg over the saddle horn, he jumped to the ground, then turned and held out his arms to Calley. She slid into them and he savored the closeness for a split second before stepping away from her.

"Do you really mean it, Matt?" she asked softly. "You'd forfeit everything?"

"I'm not going to let anything or anyone else suffer because of this stupid bet. Bud's arm is broken. Three steers are killed. A horse tortured, and maybe worse if infection sets into that hoof."

He'd told her about the razor blade he'd found wedged in the hoof of Cliff's horse, and had seen the shock and revulsion she'd felt reflected in her blue eyes. He knew she wanted to catch the person responsible as much as he did. Even if she didn't have as much to lose.

She held out her hand. "Good luck, Matt."

A pressure built in his chest as he reached out to clasp it. He was putting everything on the line now. His ranch. His dream. The pressure grew into an ache when he looked into her eyes and saw the empathy there. She knew the struggle in his heart without either one of them saying a word. It was the closest he'd ever come to perfect communion with another person before.

Without thinking of the consequences, he pulled her into his arms and kissed her. It wasn't just to satisfy his desire for her, although his body reacted whenever she was near, but for another reason entirely. A reason he couldn't explain. Gratitude, maybe. Or friendship. Or perhaps just to assuage the loneliness that had cast a shadow over his life for much too long.

The kiss was tender. Brief. Over almost as soon as it had begun. But Matt felt a shift in his soul that he didn't want to acknowledge. Not when his dream of a lifetime might be nearing its end.

Without another word, he turned and mounted his

horse. Ten minutes later he was back at the campsite. He glanced over his shoulder at the rocky outcropping, but couldn't see any sign of Calley. Then he gave a loud shout to rouse the crew.

He found Cliff already awake and cussing over by the horses. His friend found the damage to his mare's hoof and was angrier than Matt had ever seen him.

"It was a razor blade," Matt explained as the crew gathered around them. "Wedged in the hoof, just below the coronet band."

Boyd looked around the group. "Don't you suppose it's possible the horse could have picked it up accidentally?"

"Like hell," Cliff muttered, a muscle flexing in his lean jaw. "We all know this was no accident."

Matt looked at Boyd, the most likely suspect in his mind. The kid was lazy, spoiled and the kind who liked to cause trouble. "I'm afraid Calley's disappearance might not be an accident, either."

Deb Gunn paled. "Calley's missing?"

Matt nodded. "I've been up for an hour and can't find her anywhere. I already checked inside the chuck wagon and down by the river."

Boyd looked as shocked as the rest of the crew. But maybe he was just a damn good actor.

Davis rubbed his goatee. "She's got to be around here somewhere. Wouldn't she have hollered or something if somebody tried to take her?"

"Unless she didn't have a chance," Cliff said glumly.

"Well, it's not going to do her or us any good to stand around and think the worst," Deb announced. "Let's go look for her."

Matt nodded, trying to ignore the stab of guilt he

felt for deceiving his friends. He knew they'd understand once the traitor was caught.

If he was caught.

"Arnie and I will scout north of the herd," Matt
said. "Deb and Davis, you take the river."

"Boyd and I will head east," Cliff added, already
moving toward the spare horses they'd brought along
for the drive. "We won't stop until we find her.
Agreed?"

Everyone nodded, then headed silently for their
horses.

Matt climbed up into his saddle, wishing once
again that he'd declined Rufus Tupper's job offer.
Suddenly, that half a million dollars just didn't seem
worth it.

CALLEY HID behind two narrow slabs of rock, watching the activity below. She saw Matt gather the crew
together, then a few moments later, they all scattered
in different directions. The Gunns rode toward the
river, Davis crossing the shallow water to the other
side. Cliff and Boyd rode east of the herd, the land
thick with trees and brush. Matt and Arnie headed
north, mingling amid the herd so it became harder
and harder for her to see them.

Calley waited and watched, her throat tight. On the
one hand, she wanted to discover the identity of the
person responsible for these acts of cruelty. On the
other hand, if one of the crew was responsible, it
meant someone she considered a friend had betrayed
them all. Yet if the culprit wasn't apprehended, Matt
was prepared to give up everything.

As their search continued, Calley could barely see
Matt and Arnie up in front of the herd. Deb and Davis

had followed the bend of the river and were now riding out of her view. Cliff and Boyd were completely out of sight.

She leaned back against the rock, fearing this ploy wouldn't lead anywhere. That Matt would give up his dream of owning a ranch because his integrity wouldn't let him continue.

It wasn't right. And it wasn't fair.

Then she saw something that made her breath hitch in her throat. One of the crew had curled off and was now riding hell for leather in her direction. She held her breath as he rode directly below her, then past her to another outcropping of rocks behind her about five hundred feet. Two strangers on horseback waited there.

What she saw next made her want to cry.

CHAPTER TWELVE

"THIS WAY." Calley sat just behind Matt on the saddle, directing him toward the rocks. Her heart raced in her chest and she took a deep gulp of air, feeling as if she couldn't catch her breath. Anxiety clawed at her, but she pushed it aside, telling herself it was just a reaction to what she'd seen. Nothing else. She couldn't let it be anything else.

She braced her hands on his waist, feeling the tension emanating from him. When she'd realized what was happening from her perch on the outcropping, she'd scrambled down and made a run for the campsite. Then she'd furiously rung the bell to call all the crew back. She'd silently endured their exclamations of relief and endless questions until she could pull Matt aside to tell him what she'd seen.

The scene she described had made the blood drain from his face.

He'd been mostly silent since then, communicating more by the stiff carriage of his body and the starkness in his eyes than with words.

As they neared the spot, Calley pointed to a large gray rock surrounded by spindly sagebrush. "Over there."

He reined in his horse. "Maybe you should wait here."

"No." She took a deep breath, the pressure in her

lungs increasing. "I've already come this far. And you might need me."

He didn't argue with her as she'd half expected. Instead, he nudged Jericho into a slow walk, perhaps putting off the unpleasant scene ahead as long as possible.

A low moan sounded as they approached.

"Oh, my God," Calley whispered.

Cliff Donovan lay sprawled on the ground, his face covered with bruises and a large gash above his swollen right eye. He winced as he looked up at them, then turned his head away.

Matt swung off his horse and hurried to Cliff's side. "Who did this to you?"

"Nobody," Cliff muttered, dirt clinging to the perspiration on his face and neck. "I did it to myself."

Calley knelt down beside Matt. "What happened, Cliff? Who were those riders I saw?"

"Men from Lester Hobbs's crew."

Matt glanced at Calley, then back down at Cliff. "How badly are you hurt?"

"I don't think anything is broken," Cliff said, struggling to sit up. "Except my pride."

Calley and Matt each grabbed an arm to steady him, but he shook them off.

"I'm fine." Then he looked at Matt with his good left eye. "It was a setup, wasn't it? Calley was never missing."

Matt didn't say anything, just stared at his friend.

Cliff gave them a mirthless smile. "Hobbs's men said I was too damn tenderhearted for my own good. I thought they'd done something to her. Finally gone too far."

"Are you saying they're responsible for all the

problems we've had on this drive?" Matt asked, arching a brow.

After a brief hesitation, Cliff shook his head. "No. Not all of them."

"Then who is?"

Cliff's jaw tightened. "Me."

"No." Matt's denial was swift and hot.

"Yes," Cliff countered, his face grim. "Who else had access to the chuck wagon? Or knew the route we planned to take? I'm the damn traitor, Matt. The person you'd be the least likely to suspect. That's what made it so perfect, according to Hobbs."

Matt stood up, his fists clenched. "Then I hope Hobbs paid you well. Bud's broken arm should have been worth at least a few grand. Did you enjoy killing those steers? And torturing your own horse? That was a touch of genius. Especially when you played the part of enraged horse lover. You missed your calling, Donovan. You should have been an actor, 'cause you're sure a disgrace as a cowboy."

"I won't argue with you about that," Cliff replied, his tone rife with disgust. "I'm a disgrace as a man, too."

Calley stared at him. "Why did you do it?"

He met her gaze and the stark expression in his eyes made her want to weep. "Did you know my wife is expecting twins?"

She shook her head.

"One of the babies isn't the same size as the other one, so she had to go to a specialist in Tucson and have a bunch of tests done. That visit alone cost over five hundred dollars. I barely make that much in one week."

Matt's eyes narrowed. "You're blaming Katie?"

"Hell, no," Cliff retorted angrily. "I'm blaming myself. Because my kind of work doesn't come with health insurance benefits for me or my family. If there's a problem with the babies it could cost us thousands of dollars. Money I don't have. What kind of man can't pay to take care of his own family?"

Matt folded his arms across his chest. "Why didn't you come to me for help?"

"A man who can't take care of his own family isn't much of a man."

"So you went to Hobbs? Offered to do a little dirty work for him in exchange for some cash."

"He came to me," Cliff replied tersely. "Made me an offer I couldn't refuse." He looked up at Matt. "Sound familiar?"

"No one could pay me enough to injure a friend or torture an animal."

Calley looked between the two men, feeling incredibly helpless. The close bond they'd shared for so many years was shattering and there was nothing she could do to stop it.

"What happened to Bud was an accident," Cliff retorted. "I sawed through that wagon axle, but I never meant for anyone to get hurt. All I was supposed to do was delay the drive long enough for Hobbs's crew to get a good lead."

"Or kill off enough cattle so we'd lose the bet."

Cliff shook his head. "I admit I culled those three steers off from the rest of the herd, but I left them alive and well in the brush. I swear it. Hobbs's men must have done the dirty work."

"Funny how there's always someone else to blame. First, Katie's pregnancy, then Hobbs's men. I suppose you're innocent of hobbling your own horse, too."

Two red spots burned in Cliff's cheeks, but he didn't lose his temper. "Hobbs didn't think I was doing my job, since we're still at least two days ahead of his crew, despite the setbacks. He decided I needed a little incentive."

"So he hurt your horse," Calley concluded, then pointed to the gash on his head. "Is that also the reason they beat you?"

Cliff took a deep breath. "I told them today I was through. I wasn't going to play their games any longer. But that's not what they wanted to hear. I guess when their words didn't convince me to change my mind, they decided to use their fists."

Matt turned his back on Cliff. "Get the hell out of my sight."

Cliff stood up. "I know I don't deserve any favors from you, Matt, but I'm going to ask one anyway. Please don't tell my wife about this."

Matt didn't turn around or reply.

"She's got enough to worry about with the babies," Cliff continued, his voice cracking. "And I really don't want her to know what kind of man she married. I love her too much to lose her."

Tears stung Calley's eyes, but Matt appeared unmoved by Cliff's words. The stubborn set of his shoulders told her that much.

Cliff picked up his cowboy hat off the ground and slapped it against his leg to remove the dust. "Stamford is only about twenty miles to the west. I'll gather my things and walk there."

"Take the horse," Matt said, nodding to the mare grazing beside him.

"The drive can't spare another horse," Cliff countered.

"Take the damn horse!" Matt turned around to face him, his hands still fisted. "The sooner you get the hell out of my sight, the better."

Cliff stared at him for a long moment, then gave a sharp nod. "Fine. I'll take a horse. And whether you believe it or not, I want you to win this bet, Matt. I just hope someday you can forgive me for trying to make you lose it."

Calley's throat ached as she watched Cliff walk slowly back toward the camp. She knew there'd be no forgiveness for him there, either. Just cold stares and stony silence.

She turned back to Matt. "I'm sorry."

"So am I." He rubbed one hand over his chin. "You can ride Jericho back to camp."

Her brows drew together. "What about you?"

"I'll be there soon."

She understood his need to be alone, even as she ached to comfort him. But what could she possibly say? She'd lost friends before, but not because of their duplicity. Her mother had been responsible for the friendship void in Calley's life.

But then, maybe Calley was blaming someone else for her problems, just as Cliff had tried to do. Her mother might have been the catalyst, but Calley had done little to stop her, too paralyzed with fear of her own mortality.

For ten long years she'd let her mother control her life. But she couldn't blame Liv for all her problems. Leaving home had been the first step to becoming a whole person. But not the only step.

Calley knew now that she couldn't afford to wait for life to catch up with her. She had to catch up with life.

THUNDER RUMBLED across the Texas sky that night. Fearing rain, the crew had set up the pup tents. Matt had chosen to stake his tent close to the river, out of sight of the camp. He couldn't be around the crew tonight, not when all they wanted to talk about was Cliff and his betrayal.

Matt had kept his focus on the cattle drive all day, pushing the herd to make up for some of the miles they'd lost because of the delays. He'd also done his best to avoid the crew's questions and Calley's attempts at conversation. Night had fallen by the time they'd made camp that night and everyone had been exhausted. He'd learned a long time ago that hard work could shove unwelcome thoughts from his mind. That if he pushed his body to the limit, then he could numb the feelings that threatened just beneath the surface.

But now, as he tossed and turned in his bedroll long after midnight, he realized those feelings wouldn't be denied. Every time he closed his eyes, he saw Bianca's cute little pixie face. Heard Katie Donovan's infectious laugh. Cliff's family had always welcomed him with open arms, making him feel wanted. Even loved.

He struggled out of his bedroll and grabbed his jacket, then emerged from the small tent. Breathing in the crisp night air, he walked over to the river's edge. No matter how hard he tried, he couldn't get Cliff's words out of his brain. *A man who can't take care of his family isn't much of a man.*

Matt thrust his hands through his hair, inwardly cursing Cliff for not coming to him for help. At the same time, he knew that Cliff's stubborn pride matched his own. What man wanted to admit he couldn't provide for his wife and children?

Maybe that was the reason Todd Radcliffe had run out on his family all those years ago.

Scooping up a handful of pebbles off the ground, Matt started hurling them one by one into the water. His mother had never told him the reason his father had abandoned them. Or why Todd hadn't bothered to maintain contact with Matt. It had been over twenty-four years since Matt had last seen his father. And he rarely thought about him.

Until now.

Cliff's betrayal had brought back all those old, unwelcome memories. And just like when he was twelve and out in the world alone, he wondered what he should have done differently. Not only with Cliff, but with his father.

And Violet Mitchum.

He knew the answer to that question. He'd lost Violet's respect and love when he'd started that fire. Smoking one of Charles Mitchum's expensive cigars definitely hadn't been worth losing his home, or losing one of the people that had mattered most in his life. Especially when his nervous, desperate mother had remarried shortly after they'd left Pinto and moved to Chicago. Rita's new husband had made it clear that Matt wasn't welcome in the family. His stepfather had also been the one to arrange a summer job for Matt on a ranch five hundred miles away.

So Matt had never gone back. He hadn't considered the house in Chicago home anyway. Pinto, Texas, was the only place that had ever claimed that position in his heart.

Footsteps sounded on the path behind him, making

him swear sharply under his breath. The last thing he wanted was company. Especially at this time of night. He tossed the last pebble into the river, then turned to leave.

Calley stood in his way, dressed in worn blue jeans and a soft pink flannel shirt. Her silky blond hair hung down around her shoulders. Her shirt was untucked, the collar open just far enough for him to glimpse the curve of her breast. She looked fresh and young and beautiful, and it took every ounce of his fraying will-power not to pull her into his arms and lose himself and his painful memories in her sweet kiss.

"What are you doing up?"

She smiled. "I could ask you the same question."

"I'm not really in the mood to talk."

She arched a brow. "Then what are you in the mood for?"

He took a step closer to her. "You."

CHAPTER THIRTEEN

CALLEY STOOD her ground. "Is that supposed to scare me off?"

"It should." He took another step toward her. "Because I'm in no mood to talk about Cliff or how I should have forgiven him."

"I don't want to talk about Cliff, either," she said evenly, while her heart pounded double-time in her chest. When she'd seen Matt down by the river, she knew she wasn't the only one plagued with insomnia. At first she'd debated whether she should follow him. But now it was too late to turn back. "Then why are you here?" he asked.

She couldn't tell him the reason in words. So she decided to show him. His expression didn't change as she took one step toward him, then another.

"Calley," he whispered as she reached up to kiss him.

She wasn't sure if it was a plea to stop or an invitation to continue. And she didn't care.

Her mouth met his with an urgency she couldn't hide, her hands cradling his rough cheeks. His skin was warm and she let herself melt into him.

A strangled groan emanated from his throat and he broke the kiss and glared down at her. "Why the hell are you doing this to me?"

Because I want to live again. Because tomorrow

might never come and I want you to need me as much as I need you. Because I'm not going to just day-dream about love anymore. But she didn't say any of those things. She just stared up at Matt, willing him to succumb to the same emotions that had brought her to the river's edge. To the passion that had sizzled between them from almost the first moment they'd met.

She didn't know how most women conveyed their desire for a man. The art of flirting was as foreign to her as the games of courtship. She could only offer herself and hope it would be enough to entice him.

If not, then they'd both be embarrassed and Calley would be guilty of making a monumental fool of her-self. But at least she wouldn't be a coward.

Matt still didn't move, though she could see the play of muscle in his tightly held jaw. The howl of a lone coyote broke the silence of the night.

Her gaze dropped to his chest. His shirt was un-tucked and unbuttoned. Almost without thinking, she reached out to touch him, trailing her fingers through the dark hair on his chest. "Did you mean what you said before? Do you really want me, Matt?"

He swore softly, then pulled her into his arms, kiss-ing her with a fierce intensity that made her spirits soar. *He wanted her.* She could feel it in his kiss and the rapid beat of his heart beneath her fingertips. And definitely in the way his hard body pressed against her.

Then he lifted his head and stared into her eyes, as if daring her to remain in his arms. "Is that proof enough for you?"

She shook her head. "No. Prove it some more."

"Hell," he whispered, then kissed her again, more

gently this time, his tongue tracing the seam of her mouth until she opened for him.

A small moan escaped her at the silken thrust of his tongue. His hands braced her hips, pulling her firmly against him.

Calley leaned into him, relishing the way their bodies molded together. Desire, hot and delicious, unfurled deep in her belly. She wound her arms around his neck, determined not to let him go in case he was besieged by troublesome second thoughts.

But she didn't have to worry. Matt broke the kiss, then scooped her up in his arms and carried her into his tent.

Once inside, he set her gently on the bedroll. Then he knelt down and brushed a strand of hair off her cheek. "It's not too late for you to change your mind."

"But it's too late for you," she countered, reaching up to push the shirt off his shoulders. The past ten years had been spent weighing every decision. Wondering and worrying how it would affect her health. Her mother had feared any new situation, and that fear had often rubbed off on Calley. But now her fear was just the opposite—that she might miss out on something wonderful because she was too frightened to experience it.

She'd read about love. Wondered about it. Dreamed about it. But no man had every held her in his arms and made love to her.

That was all about to change.

Matt knelt before her, shirtless and magnificent. His body was heavily muscled, and she reached out to touch the firm ripples on his stomach.

He closed his eyes, his Adam's apple bobbing in his throat. "I don't think you should do that."

"Why not?" she asked, her fingers dipping beneath the waistband of his jeans.

He grabbed her wrist. "Because if you do, this moment will be over before it's begun."

Heat suffused her cheeks. The last thing she wanted was for her inexperience to show. Taking a deep breath, she reached up and began slowly unbuttoning her shirt. His sultry gaze followed her fingers, making her skin prickle with awareness. She'd been undressed in front of countless doctors in the last decade, but no man had ever looked at her like this before. So intently. So hungrily.

The raw desire on his handsome face made her feel more confident. She peeled her shirt off, then teasingly slipped one strap of her lacy white bra off her shoulder.

He swallowed hard. "Do you have any idea what you're doing to me, Calley?"

"No," she answered honestly. Then she turned to present her back to him. "Give me a hand?"

His fingers lightly caressed the curve of her spine, making her close her eyes at the delicious sensation. Then he fumbled for a moment with the clasp of her bra before it finally fell away. The cool night air hit her bare breasts, making her nipples tighten.

Matt placed his hands on her shoulders and turned her around to face him. "You are so damn beautiful."

In that moment, she felt beautiful. She leaned up to kiss him, her breasts crushing against his bare chest. He moaned under his breath, his tongue seeking hers as his fingers slid up her rib cage and brushed over one nipple.

Now it was her turn to moan as he tenderly cradled one breast in his palm, the sensation of the rough pads of his fingers driving her crazy.

Touch by touch, Matt turned her jittery apprehension into pulsing anticipation. He shed her inhibitions with the same ease as her clothes until she lay naked before him.

His clothing quickly followed hers onto the ground. Her hands moved over him, tracing the hard muscles and contours of his powerful body. She couldn't help the butterflies that invaded her stomach when her gaze swept downward.

Sensing her uneasiness, Matt took her in his arms once again, gentling her with tender kisses. Nibbling her lips and whispering how much he wanted her. How much he needed her.

Calley took a deep breath and looked up into his eyes. "Show me."

He left her a moment, fumbling for something deep inside his saddlebag. She heard the rip of foil, then the next moment, he was with her again. Matt groaned low in his throat as he kissed her, his hands caressing the length of her body. Then he moved over her.

She sucked in her breath, all too aware of her inexperience. Would he notice? Be disappointed? But as his fingers traced the delicate skin from her knee to her inner thigh, then moved to more intimate places, her worries disappeared in a whirlwind of desire. She arched against him. "Matt...please."

"Please what, Calley?" he murmured, leaning down to trail kisses over her throat.

"Please...love me."

He answered her with a scorching kiss that left her

breathless. Then he was inside her. Her breath hitched in her throat at the sharp, unexpected pain. He soothed her with tender kisses until it gradually lessened. Then he began to move and she exalted in the indescribable sensation of two bodies joining together to become one.

She brought her arms up around his neck and held on as he carried her farther and faster than she ever thought she could go. Her body arched up to meet his, matching his rhythm. She looked up into his face, amazed that she was responsible for the transformation of his stoic features.

Then she couldn't think at all anymore, but let him take her to a place she'd never been before. He followed her there, hoarsely crying her name. Then he relaxed onto her body and she held on to him, inexplicably afraid she'd lose him forever if she let him go.

"I'm crushing you," he said after a long while, lifting his head to gaze into her eyes.

"No," she whispered, holding him tighter. "Stay."

He kissed her, then relaxed against her once more, his face pressed into the crook of her neck. He didn't seem to want to leave her, either. And she knew why. Because he didn't want to face the reason they'd both been unable to sleep.

"Cliff didn't mean to hurt you," she whispered, knowing she was taking a chance. Matt might retreat into his hard shell once more. But she'd seen the raw pain in his eyes when Cliff had made his confession. And she knew from personal experience how unhealthy it was to carry that kind of pain alone. And how incredibly lonely.

"He loves you," she whispered. "No matter what."

Matt didn't say anything, his face still pressed into her neck. But she could feel the warm moisture of his tears trickling over her skin and the almost imperceptible quaking of his body.

Tears stung her eyes, too. She hugged him closer to her, realizing that Matt Radcliffe had done more than initiate her in the awesome intimacies between a man and a woman.

He'd found his way into her damaged heart.

THE NEXT MORNING, Calley hummed under her breath as she stirred the big batch of hominy grits in the cast-iron pot. The warm breeze riffled through her hair and a tingle of pleasure shot through her when she remembered the way Matt had made love to her a second time last night.

"It should be a danged crime to be so cheerful first thing in the morning," Deb Gunn grumbled as she approached the chuck wagon.

Calley grinned and poured the woman a cup of coffee, used to her early-morning crankiness. She'd noticed that Davis made a habit of steering clear of his wife until she'd downed at least two cups of coffee.

"It's going to be a beautiful day," Calley announced, handing Deb the steaming cup.

Deb snorted. "Looks like another scorcher on the way to me." She took a sip of coffee, then eyed Calley over the rim of the cup. "Speaking of scorchers, you sure were gone a long time last night."

A hot blush suffused Calley's cheeks, making any attempt at an innocent explanation impossible.

"Yep," Deb continued. "I was working night shift and saw you and Matt standing down by the river. Then next thing I knew, poof, you were gone."

"Grits?" Calley asked, picking up a serving spoon. When in trouble, change the subject.

Deb nodded, then emitted a wry chuckle. "Don't worry. Your secret is safe with me. You got good taste, Calley. Matt is the best-lookin' hunk of a man west of the Mississippi."

Calley smiled as she spooned up a dish of grits. "You're not going to get any argument from me."

"Just don't tell Davis I said so."

"Okay, you've got a deal," she replied, handing over the plate. "But since we're sharing secrets, will you tell me one thing?"

"If I can."

Calley took a deep breath. "When did you know you were in love with Davis?"

"Hell, that's easy." Deb glanced over toward their tent, where Davis was now hunched over a bucket of water, shaving cream lathered over his cheeks. "When he started a fight with a cowboy three times his size who called me the ugliest wrangler in the West."

Her eyes softened at the memory. "Davis didn't even know my name at the time. Just stepped up and threw a punch that broke the jerk's nose. Course, he got the tar beat out of him after that."

"So it was love at first sight?"

Deb smiled. "More like love at first punch. Any man who would stick up for a worn-down cowgirl like me didn't stand a chance of getting away single."

Calley looked toward the herd, watching Matt atop Jericho, slowly winding his way through the cattle.

His back was broad and straight and his shoulders wide. She felt a ridiculous swell of pride for the cowboy she so wanted to call her own. A man she didn't even know a few weeks ago. Somehow, though, she knew he'd always been out there. Waiting for her.

Deb followed her gaze. "Men like Matt don't fall easy. You've got something special, Calley. I've never seen him act this way with a woman before."

"But the cattle drive will be over in little more than a week," she replied, voicing a fear she didn't want to face. Did Matt want her forever, or just for right now? Her inexperience with men made that question impossible for her to answer.

Her friend sighed. "Then you've got just that much time to convince that stubborn cowboy that he can't live without you."

CHAPTER FOURTEEN

TWO DAYS LATER, Matt walked up to Calley. "I have a surprise for you."

She stood near the back of the chuck wagon, taking inventory of their dwindling supplies. He saw the blush rise in her cheeks when she looked up at him. They hadn't been able to snatch more than a few moments alone together since their special night. Time enough to share some sweet, stolen kisses, but nothing more.

He knew he wasn't the only one experiencing these odd, giddy feelings. He could tell by the way she sang those sappy love songs to the mules all day long that Calley was as smitten as he was.

"What kind of surprise?" she asked, looking prettier than ever in her dusty blue jeans and faded blue cotton shirt. Her hair was pulled back into a loose ponytail and her nose was sunburned and peeling.

The corner of his mouth kicked up in a smile. "If I told you, it wouldn't be a surprise, would it?"

"Are you still riding into Throckmorton this morning?"

He nodded. The cattle drive had brought them within five miles of the small Texas town. Today was one of their days off the trail, allowing the steers to rest and graze. It gave him the perfect opportunity to stock up on enough supplies to carry them the rest of the way.

"I'm leaving soon. Do you have your list ready?"

"Just about," she replied, turning back toward the chuck wagon. She climbed inside, then hunched down in front of an open trunk. "How big is Throckmorton?"

"About a thousand people, I'd guess."

"Anything more than a grocery store there?" she asked casually, her back still to him.

"Like what?"

She gave a shrug of her shoulders. "I don't know. A movie theater…a bowling alley…a pharmacy…a fast-food restaurant."

"Sounds like someone is missing city life."

She turned around. "Not at all. I was just curious."

"Well, I'll take a look around when I get there and let you know."

She tore off the top sheet of the notepad she carried, then handed her list to him. "Whatever you do, don't forget the coffee or Deb may instigate a mutiny."

He folded the paper in half, then tucked it in his pocket. "I'll make that my top priority. Or rather my second top priority."

She gave him a smile that tugged at his heart. "And what's your first?"

"It's part of the surprise. Just be ready at seven o'clock tonight."

She arched a brow, the expression in her eyes making his body tighten in anticipation. "Ready for what?"

He leaned over to kiss the tip of her nose. "You'll just have to wait and see."

Several hours later, he packed the last of the supplies into the saddlebags strapped across Jericho's back. The afternoon sun beat down on him. It baked the paved streets and sidewalks of Throckmorton, making it seem even warmer in town than it did on the range. He wiped his brow, then glanced at his watch, hoping he'd have time for a quick dip in the river before his date with Calley tonight.

"Mr. Radcliffe?"

He turned to see a middle-aged woman with ash-blond hair and eerily familiar blue eyes. "Yes?"

She held out her hand. "I'm Liv Graham. Calley's mother."

He took off his hat, then shook her hand, confused and unaccountably wary. "How do you know who I am?"

She smiled. "I found your picture in the Santa Fe newspaper. It told all about Mr. Tupper's re-creation of a historic cattle drive along the Goodnight-Loving Trail. I've been following along at a distance. When I saw that you'd camped just outside town, I took a chance that I might find you here."

"Is there a reason you've been following us?"

She squared her narrow shoulders. "I'm concerned about my daughter."

He wondered why Calley had never mentioned her mother. Then he realized she'd never talked about any family, or about her life before the cattle drive. He'd shared bits of his past and his dreams for the future with her. But Calley had been strangely silent on both subjects. Funny how he hadn't realized that until now.

"Calley is fine," he assured her. "The rules for the cattle drive prevent the use of cellular phones. Otherwise I'm sure she would have called you to let you know she was all right.''

''I'm relieved to hear it. Although, I must tell you, Mr. Radcliffe, that I'm very surprised you would hire someone in Calley's condition.''

A vague uneasiness settled over him. ''Condition?''

''She didn't tell you?''

He didn't like discussing Calley behind her back, even if it was with her mother. There was something…unsettling about Liv Graham. An intensity in her eyes that he didn't like or understand. ''If you'll excuse me, Mrs. Graham, I really need to be getting back to work.'' Then he turned toward his horse.

''She could die.''

Matt froze, then slowly turned around. ''What did you say?''

Liv took a deep breath. ''Calley has a serious heart condition. We almost lost her ten years ago. The only reason she's stayed alive this long is because I've made every effort to ensure she doesn't overexert herself or become exposed to any potentially dangerous situations.''

Denial rushed through his veins. ''She seems fine to me.''

His voice sounded much harsher than he intended, his words a barely veiled accusation that she was a liar. He didn't want to believe her. Couldn't let himself believe her. He'd lost too many people in his life already. He couldn't lose Calley, too.

Sweet, wonderful, sexy Calley. Who sang silly love songs and kissed him like he'd never been kissed before. Who had held him while he'd cried over Cliff's betrayal. Something he hadn't done since he was twelve years old.

Liv hesitated for a moment, as if weighing how much she should divulge. "I'm afraid she's not fine, Mr. Radcliffe. Her condition is called myocarditis. She's been under the intensive care of a cardiologist for the last decade." Her lower lip quivered. "I think the stress has finally gotten to her and she's just decided to give up."

"That doesn't sound like Calley," he retorted, a sickening fear slowly eroding his doubts.

Liv's face softened and he saw moisture gleam in her eyes. "She's wonderful, isn't she? So beautiful. So happy. From the moment she was born, she's been like a beacon of light in my life." Her words caught in her throat and she took a deep breath. "In fact, I simply can't imagine life without her."

"She's fine," he reiterated. "She seems fine to me. Perfectly healthy."

Liv nodded. "I know. She was fine ten years ago, too. Until one day when she fainted and her lips turned blue. We almost lost her then. The doctor made it very clear how precarious her condition could become."

He raked one hand through his hair, wishing he hadn't decided to come into Throckmorton today. Wishing Liv Graham had never tracked him down.

But would that make her story any less true?

"Calley takes medication," Liv continued. "But working out in this hot sun can't be good for her. Her heart's simply not strong enough for that kind of exertion."

Her words had the same effect as a sucker punch in the gut. If Calley was on medication, that explained her strange curiosity about the businesses in Throckmorton. He could hear her voice in his mind. *A movie theater…a bowling alley…a pharmacy…* She didn't want to see a flick or bowl, she wanted to refill a prescription.

Only he knew there wasn't a town big enough to support a drugstore until they reached Jacksboro. And that was still several days away.

"If you could just talk to her," Liv said, breaking into his thoughts. "Convince her that continuing on this cattle drive isn't in her best interest."

Her plea puzzled him. "I don't understand why you're asking this of me, Mrs. Graham. Why don't you find Calley and tell her yourself?"

She tilted her chin. "I'm sorry to say my daughter doesn't listen to me anymore. She didn't even tell me she was leaving home. One day I found her closet empty and her car gone." A lone teardrop spilled onto her cheek. "There was no note. No phone call. Nothing."

That didn't sound like Calley, either, but Matt kept that opinion to himself. He didn't know anything about Liv Graham or her relationship with her daughter. And he sure couldn't draw on any wisdom or experience from his own dysfunctional family.

"Will you do it, Mr. Radcliffe? Will you persuade Calley to come home?"

He shook his head. "Your daughter is pretty stubborn. I don't think anything I could say would convince her to abandon the cattle drive."

Her blue eyes hardened. "Then fire her."

He blinked at the harsh tone of her voice. Liv Graham reminded him of a high-strung mare. Gentle one moment, skittish the next. Perhaps the explanation was as simple as a mother's instinct to protect her young. But Matt guessed it was something more.

"She's already pulled more than her share of the workload," he said evenly. "Firing her wouldn't make any sense at all."

"So you'd rather be responsible for killing her?"

The accusation struck him straight in the heart. He couldn't imagine warm, vivacious Calley dying. Not when she'd been so alive and passionate in his arms just two nights ago. The thought of losing her made him queasy. But firing Calley simply wasn't an option. Not after everything they'd shared together.

"I'll see what I can do," he hedged.

Liv smiled, obviously confident that she'd gotten through to him. "I'm sure you'll do what's best for Calley. Believe me, Mr. Radcliffe, I know from personal experience how hard it is to keep Calley from pursuing something she wants. But if it saves her life, it's worth it."

He nodded, then put on his cowboy hat, more than ready to leave Throckmorton behind.

"Will you promise me one more thing?" she asked as she watched him unloop Jericho's reins from the hitching post.

"If I can."

"Promise me you won't tell Calley that we met here today."

He shook his head. "I don't like keeping secrets."

"It's for her own sake rather than mine, Mr. Radcliffe. She's...stubborn. If she finds out I've interfered in her life, she'll never forgive me. And I'm afraid it might lead her to take even more chances with her health." Liv reached out one hand and touched his forearm. "Please. Promise me."

He looked into blue eyes that were too damn familiar and found he couldn't refuse her. "I promise." Then he moved around to the side of his horse. "Are you planning to stay in Throckmorton?"

She shook her head. "No. I'm going back to San Antonio today and get the house ready for Calley's return."

He swung up into the saddle and took the reins in his hands. "Are you that confident she'll come home?"

She looked up at him, squinting in the glare of the sun. "I can see that you care about my daughter, Mr. Radcliffe. If you really want what's best for her, then yes, I believe she'll come home."

Matt watched as Liv turned and walked away. She had a regalness about her, a mature beauty and grace that he couldn't help but admire. No doubt Calley would be just as lovely when she reached the same age. Perhaps even more so.

If she lived that long.

He wheeled his horse around, then spurred the gelding toward the road that led out of town, refusing to let himself dwell on that possibility. Part of him still didn't want to believe that there was anything wrong with Calley's heart. Another part of him knew it accounted for her secretiveness about her life and her odd query about a pharmacy.

I've dedicated my life to living dangerously. Those playful words she'd spoken now took on an ominous new meaning. Did Calley's illness explain her zest for living? The sunny optimism that had infected every member of the cattle drive? Had she shown them all the best way to live because she knew how easy it was to die?

"No," he exclaimed aloud as he spurred Jericho into a gallop. He damn well wouldn't let her die.

No matter what he had to do to prevent it from happening.

CHAPTER FIFTEEN

AN APPRECIATIVE whistle sounded behind Calley as she emerged from the chuck wagon. She turned to see Boyd standing behind her, his gaze traveling a leisurely path over her body.

"Hot damn," he breathed, tipping up his cowboy hat.

She didn't know whether to feel insulted or flattered by his insolent admiration. For the last hour, she'd washed away the dust of the trail and worked on making herself as pretty as possible. From the expression on Boyd's face, she'd succeeded. "Is there something you need?"

"Yes, ma'am," he replied with a devilish grin. "I'm definitely a man in need at the moment. And I think you're the only woman who can satisfy me."

She laughed in spite of herself, then saw Boyd's grin fade as his gaze shifted behind her. She glanced over her shoulder to see Matt standing next to the chuck wagon, a scowl clouding his handsome face.

"Don't you have work to do?" he asked Boyd, the cool tone of his voice making the lanky cowhand take a step back.

"Calley and I were just talkin'," Boyd muttered.

Matt's eyes narrowed. "I saw exactly what you were doing. And I don't want to see it again. Is that clear?"

Boyd's mouth thinned as a high flush mottled his lean cheeks. "Perfectly."

"Good."

Without looking at Calley, Boyd strode off, his cowboy boots kicking up dust and pebbles in his path. Despite his oversize ego and adolescent arrogance, she felt a little sorry for him.

"He didn't mean any harm," she said softly.

"He's too damn cocky," Matt replied.

"Unlike you," she teased.

He took a step closer to her, then pulled her into his arms. "I don't want another man ogling my woman."

My woman. The words sent a thrill through her. She'd been a little uneasy the past couple of days, worried that she'd made too much of their night together. But now Matt held her like he didn't ever want to let her go.

"Are you ready?" he asked, his warm breath teasing the inside of her ear.

"Only if you're ready to tell me about the surprise."

He pulled back far enough to look into her eyes. "How does a night of dinner and dancing sound?"

She laughed. "Like a dream come true."

"Arnie's already agreed to cook supper for the crew. And I've got two horses saddled and ready to go."

"Go where?" She'd assumed he meant dinner over the campfire and dancing to the twangy strumming of Davis's guitar.

"Into Throckmorton. I've got reservations made at the Cowpoke Bar and Grill. Not the swankiest place in Texas, but I hear they've got good food and a juke-box.''

She breathed a wistful sigh. "You mean I can actually eat a meal I don't have to cook myself?''

"Absolutely. Two meals if you want them.'' He tenderly smoothed a knuckle over her cheek. "I think you've been working too hard. You look thin to me.''

She smiled playfully up at him. "Boyd didn't seem to think so.''

He scowled. "It would suit me just fine if we didn't mention Boyd Tupper's name for the rest of the night.''

She took a step closer to him, her hands circling his waist. "Then what do you want to talk about?''

"You.'' He gazed into her eyes, his expression making her slightly uneasy. "I want to talk about you.''

CALLEY'S UNEASINESS increased as the evening progressed. Matt had grown quiet during the ride into town, and more than once she'd caught him looking at her. Normally, she'd be flattered by the attention, but he wasn't looking at her like a man consumed with passion. He was looking at her as if she were a jigsaw puzzle that he couldn't quite figure out how to put together.

Seated now in a secluded corner table at the Cow-poke, they both ordered steaks with a baked potato and a garden salad. After the waitress took the order, an uncomfortable silence settled between them.

"Is something wrong, Matt?'' she asked, wondering if he was still upset about Boyd. It didn't seem likely, but she couldn't figure out anything else that explained his mood.

"No," he replied, fingering one of the cracker packages in the basket on the table.

The waitress approached with their salads, preventing her from pursuing the subject. Matt picked up his fork and dug into his food.

"You eat like a man who hasn't had a decent meal in weeks," she teased, hoping to coax a smile from him.

He hesitated, his fork halfway to his mouth. Then he grinned. "Well, nothing can compare with Calley's Special Trail Wraps, but this isn't half-bad."

She laughed, then picked up her fork. He seemed fine now, making her wonder if she'd imagined his behavior before. It must be the giddiness of sharing a private dinner with Matt. A wry smile curved her mouth when she realized they'd approached their courtship backward. She'd already made love to the man, but this was officially their first date.

Calley picked and poked at her salad, realizing she wasn't the least bit hungry. The anticipation of Matt's surprise, coupled with her nervousness about their date together, had filled her stomach with butterflies. Especially when she envisioned how their night might end.

He scowled down at her salad plate. "Aren't you going to eat?"

"I think I'll wait for the steak." She pushed her plate toward him. "Go ahead and eat it if you'd like."

He looked up at her. "Is something wrong?"

"No," she replied, a little taken back by the strident tone of his voice. "I'm just not all that hungry."

The waitress's arrival forestalled Matt's reply. She set a sizzling steak platter in front of each of them. Calley picked up the salt shaker and liberally sprinkled salt over her baked potato. "This looks wonderful."

Matt nodded as he picked up his knife and fork. They ate in awkward silence, Calley all too aware of Matt's watchful gaze on her. She forced down every bite of her steak and potato, wondering why he was suddenly so concerned about her eating habits. Exactly where had this date taken a wrong turn?

"Care to dance?" she asked, determined to find a way to get it back on track. They'd had so few opportunities to be alone together, she didn't want to waste a single moment.

He gave a brisk nod, then got up and walked over to the jukebox. She watched him insert some coins into the machine, then make his selections.

A lively country-and-western song came over the speakers as Matt returned to the table and held out his hand. She took it and rose to her feet, then let him pull her into his arms for a Texas two-step.

Calley was surprised at how easily he moved about the dance floor. Despite his life on the range, it was obvious he'd done his share of dancing. Which only served to remind Calley that she wasn't the first woman in his life and probably wouldn't be the last.

She missed a step, stumbling over one of his cowboy boots. "Oops. Sorry about that."

"No problem," he said, his strong arms holding her firmly against him.

His jaw was clean-shaven and she inhaled the manly scent of his aftershave. Their feet moved smoothly over the sawdust on the dance floor, their bodies swaying to the rhythm of the music in perfect unison. It reminded her of how perfectly they'd moved together two nights ago. Had it been as special for him as it had for her? Or was she just one more partner in the dance of life?

As the music wound down, Calley mentally chastised herself for such thoughts. She'd vowed never to worry about the future, just to live for the day. And since this was one of the better days of her life, she intended to enjoy it.

Matt spun her around twice to end their dance, causing Calley to erupt into breathless laughter as she collapsed against him. He pulled her close, her back against his broad chest and his arms wrapped around her waist.

"You dance even better than you cook," he murmured, his cheek rubbing against hers.

"I think there's a compliment in there somewhere," she murmured, sighing softly as he nuzzled her neck. "But I probably don't want to look too close to find it."

Another country-and-western song came over the jukebox, this one slow and sultry. Matt turned her around in his arms, then pulled her close.

"Do you realize we're the only ones dancing?" she asked, gazing up into his dark eyes.

"Nope. I don't see anybody but you."

She smiled to herself as she laid her head on his shoulder and let the music carry her away. This was what she'd been missing for the last ten years. This completeness. More than a melding of bodies and hearts—a mingling of souls. She looked up into Matt's face as the music ended, and said the first words that came to her mind. "I think I'm falling in love with you."

He hesitated, then visibly swallowed. "I have a proposition for you."

She smiled. "Now that sounds intriguing."

He reached out and tucked a stray curl behind her ear. "I want you to go on ahead to Jacksboro."

Her brow crinkled. "What do you mean?"

"I found out there's a bus that stops at the gas station here in town at eight o'clock every morning. You could stay here in the motel tonight, then catch the bus tomorrow."

Calley stiffened, his words worse than a splash of cold water on her vulnerable heart. "Why would I want to leave the cattle drive and go to Jacksboro without you?" She didn't ask the question burning in the back of her throat: *Why would you want me to?*

He shrugged, looking distinctly uncomfortable. It didn't make her feel any better. Calley suddenly realized how inappropriate her declaration of love had been. They'd only known each other for a few weeks. He must think she was a lovesick fool to make more of their time together than it had obviously meant to him.

Yet they'd shared more in those weeks than she'd ever shared with anyone.

She closed her eyes, humiliated by the way she'd let her lack of experience show.

"Are you all right?" he asked, tipping up her chin with his finger.

She opened her eyes and took a deep breath. "Fine. And I have no intention of arriving in Jacksboro on a bus. We have a deal, remember?"

"Of course I remember. And I always keep my word."

She opened her mouth to call him on it, then she realized Matt Radcliffe hadn't promised her anything. She'd gone to him two nights ago with no expectations for the future. No declarations of love on his part. In fact, he'd initially tried to push her away.

"But I want to propose a new deal," he continued. "If you agree to leave the cattle drive, I'll go to Finders Keepers as soon as it's over."

"Why are you so anxious to get rid of me?"

His arms dropped to his side. "Because you don't belong here."

Calley didn't think she could be hurt any more. She'd been wrong.

Her throat grew so tight she had to swallow to get the words out. "Are you firing me?"

"I'm hoping you won't make me go that far."

She stepped away from him. "Well, sorry to disappoint you, cowboy. I'm not going anywhere." Despite the sting to her heart, her pride was still somewhat intact. And she intended to keep it that way. "I happen to be a woman of my word, and I promised to stick with the cattle drive to the end."

His eyes narrowed. "And if I don't want you there?"

Calley pulled away from him and focused on the door. She hoped she could make it outside before the tears started to fall. "Don't worry. I'll stay completely out of your way."

CHAPTER SIXTEEN

HE'D BLOWN IT. Big time. Three days after their disastrous date at the Cowpoke, Matt could barely get Calley to look at him, much less talk to him. And his plan to make certain she didn't overexert herself had backfired. She seemed to be working harder than ever just to prove a point.

He sat on top of his horse and watched her unhitch the mules, unable to make out the words she spoke to Samson. At least she was still talking to somebody around here. She'd lost the old straw hat she always wore somewhere along the trail. Her hair hung in two limp braids over her shoulders and her upturned face looked sunburnt.

The rest of the crew had gathered under a stand of mesquite trees, enjoying the only bit of shade for miles. An unseasonable heat wave had descended upon them, taking its toll on the cattle, and showed no signs of abating. They'd made poor progress today, barely covering eight miles. He wished they were closer to the Lazy R. Closer to a doctor in case Calley needed help.

Despite her apparent good health, he kept having visions of her collapsing. Of watching helplessly as she died in his arms. The image made his gut tighten and his own heart squeeze painfully in his chest, signaling a serious condition of his own. One he'd never suffered from before.

He'd fallen in love.

His hands tightened on the reins as he watched Calley lift two buckets and head toward the river. He climbed off Jericho, hitched the reins to a low-hanging tree branch, then ran after her. She'd already filled both buckets when he caught up with her at the riverbank.

"Let me take those."

She turned and brushed past him, not even making eye contact. "I'm fine."

He watched her walk away, wondering if that incredible night they'd shared together had only been a dream. He'd tried to protect her and lost her instead. It also bothered him more and more that she hadn't trusted him with the truth. He'd shared his dreams with her. His pain over Cliff's betrayal. But she'd revealed nothing. And he'd be damned if he was going to force her.

With a frustrated oath, he walked back to his horse. Deb Gunn met him halfway, a scowl on her weathered face.

"What the hell did you do to that girl?" she asked without preamble.

"I didn't do anything to her."

"Bullshit. She's singing love songs one day and moping around the next. And you haven't exactly been a barrel of sunshine either, Matt."

His eyes narrowed. "Since when was I ever a barrel of sunshine?"

"Good point," she retorted. "Calley Graham is the best thing that ever happened to you. And now you're doing your best to drive her away. Do you mind telling me why?''

He looked out over the horizon. ''I have my reasons.''

''In other words, you're too dumb to know any better.'' She shook her head. ''How men ever manage to snag any woman is a mystery to me. Especially when they keep most of their brains in their saddle.''

''You just worry about Davis and the cattle,'' he said coolly. ''I'll take care of Calley.''

''You're doing a damn poor job of it from where I stand. Hell, if you're not more careful, Boyd's going to jump your claim.''

''He's just a kid,'' Matt said tersely.

''That kid is man enough to know how to catch a woman on the rebound,'' Deb retorted. ''Haven't you seen the way he manages to find a seat next to Calley every night at supper? How he lingers around the chuck wagon and helps her with the dishes—hanging around long after everyone else heads off to bed.''

Matt had noticed. But he'd been too worried about Calley's health to consider Boyd a romantic rival.

Or had he been too worried about himself?

He mounted his horse, then rode away without another word to Deb. He galloped into the open range, leaving the herd and crew far behind. What he needed was time to think. Time to figure out if he was more concerned about Calley's heart…or his own.

CALLEY DISHED UP a plate of red beans and rice as Deb approached the chuck wagon. She'd seen the older woman talking with Matt, then watched him gallop off into the sunset. ''Looks like you managed to chase Matt away.''

"You and me both," Deb replied, reaching for a fork and spoon.

Calley stiffened. "I'm just trying to make him happy."

"Bullshit. The man obviously said something that rubbed you the wrong way and now you're making him suffer for it. You're doing a hell of a job, too. Matt is miserable."

Denial burned in her throat. "If he's miserable, it's because I'm still hanging around. He wanted me to leave the cattle drive."

Deb arched a brow. "Why?"

"You know more about men than I do. You tell me."

"Maybe because you scare him."

"Oh, I scared him all right," Calley said, emitting a mirthless laugh. "Made the monumental mistake of telling him I was falling in love with him. Practically the next words out of his mouth were a suggestion that I hop on the next bus. I don't think he could have made his feelings any clearer."

"Did I ever tell you about the night Davis and I got engaged?"

Calley smiled in spite of her mood. She enjoyed Deb's stories about her unorthodox courtship with Davis. "I don't think I've heard that one yet."

"Good. Now sit down there and get comfortable." Deb pointed to an empty crate, then pulled up another one and sat next to Calley. "It was about five years ago, but it still seems like yesterday to me. We were punching cows in Laredo."

"Punching cows?" Calley echoed, envisioning some kind of bovine boxing match.

"That's cowboy slang for herding cattle." Deb

took off her battered cowboy hat and ruffled her short hair with her fingers. "Anyhow, Davis and I had been going together for about three months, but we weren't going anywhere, if you know what I mean."

"I think I do."

"Well, I was tired of waiting for that man to make his move. Tackled him right outside of his bunkhouse and made it clear that I didn't want to sleep alone."

Calley bit back a smile, easily imagining the look on the face of shy Davis. "So what did he do?"

"Made up some lame excuse about how he didn't want to sully my reputation. Said he was too much of a gentleman to take any woman to bed who wasn't his wife."

"So what did you do?"

Deb grinned. "I told him I accepted his proposal. Then I took off to find a preacher. We were married the next day."

Calley laughed. "Poor Davis didn't even see it coming, did he?"

"Nope," Deb agreed, still smiling. "And that's exactly my point about you and Matt. Most men are just too dumb to know what's good for them. That's why it's up to us women to steer them in the right direction."

Calley's smile faded as she looked over the horizon. Matt still hadn't returned. "And if he's running the other way?"

"Then I guess you have to figure out a way to catch him," Deb said with a shrug.

Calley shook her head. "Matt never made me any promises. How do I know I'm just not another conquest? You told me yourself that he's a loner. Never staying in one place long enough to get attached."

"And I've never seen him act this way around another woman, either. He's testy, sullen and just itchin' for a reason to knock that sweet-talking Boyd on his rear end." Deb chuckled. "I'd say it's definitely love."

Despite Deb's success with Davis, Calley wondered if the woman really had any more experience with men than she did. Matt had made it perfectly clear that he wanted her gone.

And so far he hadn't done or said anything to make her believe he'd changed his mind.

THREE DAYS LATER, Matt lingered over a cup of coffee as he watched Calley scrape off the lunch plates. The rest of the crew had mounted their horses ready to drive the reluctant cattle out of the cool river.

The day was the hottest yet, the temperature climbing into the upper eighties. The hot sun made the cattle sluggish and the crew short-tempered. He'd sent Boyd ahead to scout the trail to the Lazy R just to get a break from his constant complaining about the heat.

At least, that's the reason he gave the crew. He didn't care to admit to them that he wanted to get the guy away from Calley. He hadn't been able to enjoy a meal for the last week. Not with Tupper's nephew making the moves on his woman.

His woman.

Matt saw Calley disappear inside the chuck wagon. His suggestion that she leave the cattle drive had been motivated by concern for her health. And by something else. *Fear.* Matt hadn't wanted to face it, but that didn't make it any less true. He'd fallen in love with her sweet, sexy spirit and found himself looking forward to seeing her smiling face every morning. The thought of losing her had been unbearable, so he'd tried to push her away instead.

They'd barely spoken in the last week. But Calley hadn't left his thoughts. Or his heart. Matt had never been a coward before. And he wasn't about to start now.

He dumped the rest of his coffee on the ground, then strode toward the chuck wagon. He'd already wasted five precious days. He wasn't about to waste a moment more.

The sound of hoofbeats made him turn around. Boyd rode into the camp at full gallop, kicking up a cloud of dust. Then he reined his horse to a quick halt, pulling off his cowboy hat to swipe the perspiration off his forehead.

"How's the trail look?" Matt asked.

"Perfect." Boyd grinned. "We're close, Matt. If we get a good start this afternoon, we should easily reach the Lazy R by suppertime."

Matt picked up one of the water buckets and hauled it over to Boyd's horse. Foam rimmed its mouth and its flanks heaved with exertion. "You shouldn't push a horse in this kind of heat."

"Jasper's fine," Boyd exclaimed, reaching down to pat his horse's neck. "We've just been riding a long time. I decided to check on the progress of Lester Hobbs's herd."

Matt frowned. "Against my orders?"

"Hell, Matt, we want to win, don't we? And we've got a good shot, too. Hobbs's herd is at least an hour behind us, maybe two."

"Did they see you?"

Boyd shook his head. "I didn't see them, either.

But their cattle kicked up enough dust to make them visible for a mile. I'm guessing they know how far we've come, too, and are making a big push to catch up."

"They'll end up killing cattle in this heat if they do."

"Hobbs isn't stupid enough to do that. But he is determined to win this thing."

Matt wanted to win, too. His dream was literally only a few hours away. Then he could leave Tupper and this silly bet behind him. He'd have a ranch to buy. And a new life to build. A life with Calley, if she'd have him.

Matt nodded toward the river. "Go report to the crew. We'll head out in fifteen minutes. Give the cattle plenty of time to get their fill of water before we do." He took the empty bucket away from the horse. "And get a different mount for the rest of the trip. Your horse has done enough work for one day."

Boyd nodded, then rode away with a boisterous holler that was sure to catch the crew's attention.

Matt had fifteen minutes to convince Calley he didn't want her to leave. He wanted her to stay with him. Forever.

But the words died in his throat when he reached the back of the chuck wagon. Calley lay crumpled on the rough, wooden floorboards of the wagon, pale as death and unconscious.

His time had just run out.

CHAPTER SEVENTEEN

CALLEY HEARD the sound of voices floating somewhere far above her.

We can't wait…hospital…so pale…fluttery pulse…hope it's not too late…

She forced her heavy eyelids open, her mind spinning as she squinted against the brightness of the sun. Black spots danced in her eyes and long shadows hovered above her. It took her a moment to recognize them. They were her friends: Deb, Davis, Boyd and Arnie.

Then she tilted her head back and saw the face of the man who was more than a friend. The man she loved—Matt.

He sat on the ground, her head cradled in his lap and his face drawn.

She tried to speak, but found her mouth dry as dust. She swallowed twice, then croaked, "What's wrong?"

"She's awake," Deb announced, kneeling down beside her. "You okay, honey?"

She struggled to rise, but Matt's hands held her shoulders firmly in place.

"Don't try to get up." He sounded different. Hoarse. As if he'd been shouting.

Calley closed her eyes and tried to remember exactly what had happened. She'd been gathering up the lunch plates, a headache pounding in her temple. The nausea she'd been fighting all morning had gotten worse, so she'd decided to lie down in the chuck wagon for a few minutes. The rest was a blank.

"How do you feel?" Matt asked, his fingers stroking the damp hair off her cheeks.

"Dizzy," she replied honestly. "A little weak."

He looked up at the crew. "No more arguments. I'm taking her into the hospital in Jacksboro."

"No," Calley protested, trying to sit up again. A wave of dizziness overcame her and she slumped back down on the ground, her head threatening to split open. She took a deep breath, then another, her heart racing in her chest. It was like the last time. Dizziness. Pounding heart. The feeling that something wasn't right inside her.

Deb held a flask of water to her lips and Calley took a few weak sips. She couldn't seem to catch her breath.

"What about the cattle drive?" Boyd said. "It'll take you at least an hour to ride into Jacksboro. And that doesn't even count the time at the hospital or the trip back. Hobbs will overtake us by then. You'll lose the bet."

Calley opened her eyes. "I'll be fine," she insisted, more out of hope than certainty. Whatever happened, she couldn't be the reason Matt lost his ranch. Not when she'd known the risks going into this adventure.

She licked her parched lips. "Just go on without me. I'll catch up with you when I'm feeling a little better."

Matt looked up at the crew. "Davis, you're in charge of the drive. Take the herd into the Lazy R and wait for us there. Deb, get my horse."

She ran off toward the makeshift corral.

Calley shook her head, despair welling inside her. "Don't do this, Matt. They need you."

"I need you," he countered, lifting her up into his powerful arms.

She was too weak to protest, her body sagging against his broad chest. Tears pricked her eyes as Deb brought his horse around. She didn't want Matt to remember her like this. Weak as a kitten and unable to stand on her own. Her throat grew thick as he handed her into Davis's wiry arms, then mounted his horse.

Davis handed her to Matt again, as if she were little more than a rag doll. Matt cradled her in his lap on the saddle, his arms on either side of her. He wound the reins around his left hand, his right hand holding her body steady against him.

"We'll keep supper warm for both of you," Deb promised, injecting a note of cheerfulness in her strained voice, "and the champagne on ice. The celebration will begin as soon as you meet us at the Lazy R."

Matt nodded, though Calley could see that his face was grim. Then she felt his powerful thighs flex beneath her as he spurred Jericho forward.

She held on to Matt, her hands curled around the fabric of his damp shirt. "Go back," she pleaded, as the campsite and the herd slowly receded behind them. "I don't want to be the reason you lose the bet."

"I don't give a damn about any bet," he said, a muscle flexing along the line of his jaw. "It's you I care about, Calley. You I love."

"You're just saying that," she countered, her heart

beating a rapid tattoo in her chest. "Because you think I'm dying."

"You're not dying." He looked down at her. "I won't let you die. Not when it took me so long to find you."

"I have a bad heart," she admitted at last.

"I know. Your mother tracked me down in Throckmorton."

She sighed. "I should have known."

"I heard all about your heart and how dangerous it was for you to be working on the cattle drive. She told me you could even…" His voice trailed off and she could feel his whole body tense.

"She told you I could die at any moment." Calley didn't need to read his mind to finish the sentence. It had been her mother's mantra for the last ten years. She knew it by heart. "Is that why you wanted to get rid of me?"

"I never wanted to get rid of you," he replied, his arm tightening around her. "I wanted to protect you. If anything happens to you…"

"It will be my own fault," she said firmly. "Not yours. Don't you see, Matt? I don't want to spend the rest of my life dying. I want to spend it living. To see something of the world. To finally experience things I've only dreamed about…like love. And no matter what happens, I'll never regret it."

"I'll tell you what's going to happen," he said, his eyes dark and fierce. "You're going to get better. Then I'm going to marry you. I'll buy a small ranch somewhere with the money Tupper is paying me and we'll have the best damn life you can imagine."

She smiled at the beautiful future he painted. "That

sounds wonderful. I just wish you'd said it before you thought I was dying.''

''I'm saying it now,'' he replied, his voice rough with tenderness. ''Marry me, Calley.''

''You're a man of your word,'' she reminded him, fighting off another wave of dizziness. ''If I say yes, you can't back out.''

''Then say yes.''

She took a deep breath, a tumult of emotions warring within her. It wasn't fair to trap Matt into a life of uncertainty. Wasn't fair to take advantage of this moment, when his fears for her were probably clouding his common sense. But life hadn't been fair to her, either. And she was just selfish enough to grab on to the beautiful dream he offered her. She might not live long enough to see it become reality, but she could hold it in her heart.

''Yes,'' she whispered. ''I'll marry you.''

MATT IGNORED the honks of the vehicles along the main drag of Jacksboro as he maneuvered his horse between lanes of traffic. He'd wasted precious minutes stopping to ask for directions to the hospital. Time Calley had spent drifting in and out of consciousness.

He'd considered calling an ambulance until he learned the hospital was only a few blocks away. Determined to get her there as quickly as possible, he spurred Jericho down the paved street, holding Calley tightly against him.

''Please, God, let her live,'' he murmured as Jericho trotted into the hospital parking lot. Matt had repeated the prayer over and over, as much to rein in his burgeoning panic as a plea to the heavens above.

She shifted in his arms as he pulled Jericho to a halt, then her eyes fluttered open.

"We're here," he said, brushing a damp tendril off her clammy brow. "Can you stand?"

"I can try."

He held on to her arm as she slid slowly off the saddle and onto the ground. When she wobbled on her feet, he jumped down to steady her. Then he looped the reins around a gas meter next to the building and left Jericho to graze in the lush grass.

Before she could take another step, he scooped her up into his arms again.

"I can walk," she protested as he strode toward the double doors of the emergency room.

"You need to save your strength for walking down the aisle, remember?"

She gave him a fleeting smile, then her head bobbed against his shoulder, her hand feebly clutching his shirt.

He was running now. As he approached the automatic doors of the hospital, they swung open and he was met by an icy blast of air. It sent a chill down his spine. Or maybe it was the way Calley was gazing up at him now. Like it might be for the last time.

"I need some help here," Matt shouted, heading toward the reception area.

A middle-aged woman in a floral lab coat sat behind a computer terminal at the counter. She pressed a button on an intercom and moments later two nurses pushing a gurney came out into the receiving area.

"My name is Maria," said the younger nurse. "Can you tell us what happened?"

Matt laid Calley gently on the gurney. "She collapsed about an hour ago. I think it might be her heart. She has a heart condition."

"Are you her husband?" the older nurse asked, peering at him over her steel-rimmed bifocals.

"No," Matt replied, staring down at Calley's lifeless body. "I'm her fiancé."

Maria rolled the gurney with Calley out of sight while the other nurse steered Matt toward the receptionist. "Sue will need some information about the patient. We'll let you know what's happening as soon as the doctor arrives."

Matt watched her walk away, torn between going after Calley or obeying her orders.

"The patient's full name, please," the receptionist asked, her fingers busily pecking the keyboard.

With a last look down the hallway where Calley had disappeared, Matt walked reluctantly over to the counter and sat in a chair. "Her name is Calley. Calley Graham."

"Address?"

He hesitated. "I'm not sure. She lives somewhere in San Antonio, Texas."

The receptionist looked up at him, both eyebrows arched. "You're her fiancé?"

"Yes." He glanced over his shoulder at the empty hallway. "Is the doctor here yet?"

"I'm certain he's on his way, Mr—" The receptionist's fingers hovered over the keyboard. "Your name, sir?"

"Radcliffe. Matthew Radcliffe."

"Do you happen to know if Miss Graham has health insurance, Mr. Radcliffe? Specifically a company name and policy number?"

He shook his head, raking his fingers through his hair. She had to be all right. She just had to be.

The receptionist punched a button on the intercom. "Maria, is the patient conscious?"

"Yes," came Maria's voice over the intercom.

Matt slumped back in his chair. That was good news at least.

"Can you ask her if she has an insurance card with her?"

Matt stared at the woman. "She could be in there dying and you're worried about her damn insurance!"

"I'm just doing my job, Mr. Radcliffe," she replied evenly. "If the patient isn't insured, we have a different system of registration."

Maria's voice sounded over the intercom again. "No card, but she said she's got insurance with the Providence Company through her father, Walter Graham."

"Thanks." The receptionist turned her chair around to the telephone and picked up the receiver.

Matt watched as she punched in an 800 number.

"This is Holling Memorial Hospital," Sue said. "We have a patient here by the name of Calley Graham, a dependent of Walter Graham. Could you please check your records and give me her policy number?"

Matt closed his eyes, certain this had to be a nightmare. He might never see Calley again, and instead of being with her, he was stuck out here with a stranger. A woman whose main concern seemed to be whether the hospital would receive its money for services rendered.

He stood up and started to pace across the shiny linoleum floor. After what seemed like an eternity, he looked up to see the younger nurse named Maria walking toward him. He tried to read the expression on her face, but time and experience had obviously made her immune to emergency situations. She seemed neither happy nor sad. Just frighteningly stoic.

"You can see her now," Maria said softly.

CHAPTER EIGHTEEN

A LUMP ROSE in Calley's throat when Matt walked into her view. She lay in a hospital bed dressed in an ugly, generic blue hospital gown that tied in the back. A thin cotton sheet covered her and an IV line was strapped to her left wrist.

He walked up to the bed, his black cowboy hat in his hands. From the way the brim was crushed between his fingers, she was surprised it was still in one piece.

She smiled up at him. "Hi."

He stepped closer to her, his dark eyes full of concern. "How do you feel?"

"Better."

Matt's gaze moved to the doctor who stood at the foot of the bed. The doctor scribbled a few notes onto a clipboard, then looked up at Matt and held out his hand. "Hello there, I'm Dr. Barnes."

Matt walked over and shook his hand. "Matt Radcliffe. How's Calley?"

"I take it you're Calley's fiancé?"

She felt a warm glow deep inside of her. "Fiancé?"

Matt turned to look at her. "Please tell me you remember accepting my marriage proposal."

She smiled. "Vaguely."

He walked closer to the bed and reached for her hand. "You said yes. And I'm holding you to it."

"Some might say I was delirious at the time," she teased. "Heat exhaustion can do that to a person."

Matt looked up in surprise. "Heat exhaustion? You mean it wasn't her heart?"

The doctor shook his head. "Calley told me about her heart condition. But I did a few preliminary tests and they all pointed to heat exhaustion. Too much sun and over-exertion. Not surprising for someone who isn't used to a lot of physical activity."

The tension in his stance eased. "So it's nothing serious?"

"Heat exhaustion is always serious," Dr. Barnes countered. "It can lead to heat stroke. She had all the classic symptoms—dizziness, headache, nausea, fainting. The combination of increased body temperature, dehydration and loss of body salts can wreak havoc if not caught soon enough. Fortunately, you brought Calley here in time to avoid any serious complications."

Matt tenderly squeezed her hand. "I knew you were working too hard."

"The IV will get some vital fluids and electrolytes into her body." Dr. Barnes reached for the clipboard. "But she should still take it easy for the next few days. Stay inside where it's cool and drink lots of fluids."

Matt nodded. "I'll see to it."

She could tell by the tone of his voice that this time Matt would brook no argument. But she didn't mind following the doctor's orders. Not when she'd be spending that time with Matt. They both deserved some days off after the grueling weeks of the cattle drive.

"Are you on any medication?" Dr. Barnes asked her, looking up from the clipboard.

"Yes," Calley replied. "My cardiologist prescribed it for my heart. But I ran out a couple of weeks ago."

"You what?" Matt's voice was low, but she could tell he was far from calm.

"We were on the trail," she explained. "Not a drugstore in sight."

"Damn it, Calley! No job is worth that kind of risk. You should have told me."

"What's the name of the medication?" Dr. Barnes interjected, pulling a prescription pad out of the pocket of his lab coat. "I can get you a temporary supply from the hospital pharmacy."

"Zenate," Calley replied.

The doctor looked up from his pad. "Are you sure?"

She nodded. "Positive. I've been taking it every day for the last six months."

He scribbled a few lines over the form, then tore it off and handed it to the nurse. "See that it's ready before Miss Graham is released."

The nurse nodded, then left the room.

Dr. Barnes replaced the pen in his pocket. "When's the last time you saw your cardiologist, Miss Graham?"

She shrugged. "It's been six months."

He nodded. "I think it might be a good idea to make an appointment for a full examination. I can contact one of the cardiologists on staff here if you wish."

Matt's brow furrowed. "What's wrong?"

"Nothing at the moment," Dr. Barnes assured him. "It's just that a patient with Calley's condition needs to be under close medical supervision. I have a number of questions that I feel a cardiologist would best be able to answer."

Calley swallowed a groan. The last thing she wanted to do was spend her time being poked and prodded. She'd suffered enough of that to last a lifetime. "I'd really rather see my own cardiologist in San Antonio—Dr. Rice."

Dr. Barnes nodded. "I'll have the hospital send him my report."

"But is it safe to wait that long?" Matt asked, concern etched on his handsome face.

Dr. Barnes smiled. "Don't worry. You take good care of Calley and she'll be just fine." Then he gave Calley a wink before walking out of the room and pulling the curtain shut behind him.

"Alone at last." Calley turned back to Matt. "I thought he'd never leave. If you don't kiss me, I may just pass out again."

He smiled. "We can't have that." Then he bent down and placed a gentle kiss on her lips.

Before he could pull away, Calley wrapped her arms around his neck and kissed him with all the love and passion she had inside her. The relief that she hadn't suffered a serious setback in her condition was almost overwhelming.

He groaned low in his throat as she deepened the kiss, using her tongue to seduce his mouth and her hands to inflame his body.

They were both breathing hard by the time he lifted his head. His dark eyes blazed with desire as he looked down at her. "The doctor said you were supposed to take it easy."

"I know. But he said sex wouldn't hurt me."

Matt's eyes widened. "You asked him?"

She nodded. "Right before you came in. That's how he guessed you were my fiancé. I thought we should know before we made hotel reservations."

A slow smile tipped up one corner of his mouth. "What exactly do you have in mind?"

"A private celebration at the fanciest hotel in Jacksboro."

"We do have a lot to celebrate," he said huskily, tracing one knuckle down her cheek.

"That's right," she agreed. "Winning the cattle drive. Our engagement."

"Your life." Matt swallowed. "I don't want to think about what would have happened if—"

She cut off his next words by placing one finger over his lips. "Then don't. Let's live for today, Matt, and not worry about tomorrow."

"Deal." He leaned over and kissed her forehead. "I love you, Calley."

The nurse pulled back the curtain and walked into the room. "You're all set to go," she announced, shutting off the IV drip, then removing the tubing from Calley's arm. "I've got your prescription waiting at the reception desk, along with your release papers. All you have to do is sign them and you can go home."

"The first stop is the Lazy R ranch," Calley said, pulling back the sheet and swinging her legs over the side of the bed. She stood up, her knees still a little shaky. "So you can collect your prize."

"Oh," the nurse said, turning to Matt. "Did you win something?"

"Yes," he replied huskily, looking into Calley's eyes. "I did."

TWO HOURS LATER, Matt could hear the sounds of a party as he rode past the front stone gate of the Lazy R ranch. Calley sat behind him in the saddle, her arms wrapped around his waist and her head resting on his back. The day's events had drained her, but that kiss they'd shared had made him anxious to get this business with Tupper over so they could return to their hotel room in Jacksboro.

They'd stopped to register for a room on their way out of town, both acting like two giddy teenagers. Matt had never felt like this before, as if he were floating two feet off the ground.

"Well, look who finally decided to show up," Davis shouted, waving a champagne bottle above his head. "We did it, Matt. Proved we're the best damn wranglers in the West."

Matt helped Calley off his horse, then climbed down from the saddle. A young cowboy from the Lazy R waited to take Jericho to the stable. Matt handed the reins to the gangly kid, then reached for Calley's hand. "Is Tupper here?"

"He got here about two hours ago." Davis hitched his thumb over his shoulder. "He's in the house now, divvying out those nice fat paychecks to all the crew. Deb's got ours." Davis looked sheepish. "I wanted to use some of the money to buy her a real diamond wedding ring, but she said we've got to use good sense and put it in our savings account."

Calley smiled. "Davis, you are a true romantic."

A hot blush suffused Davis's grizzled face, then he pointed to Matt and Calley's linked hands. "Looks like I'm not the only one."

Matt turned to her. "Should we tell him?"

"Let's wait until the crew is all together."

He nodded. "You go round them up while I track down Tupper. We'll meet by the barbecue pit." He took a step toward the house, then turned back to her. "Are you sure you feel all right?"

She rose up on her toes to kiss him. "Better every minute."

Matt watched her walk away, amazed again that someone like Calley could actually love a cranky cowboy like him. Then he turned and strode toward the sprawling ranch house.

The Lazy R was just one of many ranches owned by Rufus Tupper. He collected them like other people collected stamps. At one time, Matt had considered an offer to work as foreman at the Lazy R, overseeing the breeding of champion quarter horses. But the pay was mediocre and the benefits almost nonexistent. Besides, working for Tupper left a bad taste in his mouth. He'd endured it for the last month just because it was the only way he could ever hope to buy a ranch of his own.

The front door opened as he skipped up the steps. Marla stood in the doorway, one hand on her hip. "I thought you'd never get here."

"Something came up." He took off his hat. "Is Tupper around?"

"He's waiting for you in his study."

Matt noted the shadows under Marla's eyes and the fact that she seemed even thinner than before. Then he took a step closer to her and asked softly, ''The question is, why are you still here?''

She swallowed. ''Where else do I have to go? You didn't want me. And I'm not going back to dancing on tabletops in some run-down bar.''

''So do something else. Isn't there anything you've ever dreamed about?''

She shrugged. ''Maybe. I've always wanted to be a beautician. You know, 'cause I'm good with hair and makeup. And I like to make other people look good.''

''So why don't you do it?''

''Because it costs $9,350 to pay for tuition at a decent beauty school and I just don't have that kind of money.''

Matt was surprised at the defensiveness he heard in her voice. And by the fact that she'd obviously looked into it. He knew how it felt to have a dream that seemed out of reach. The hopelessness that never seemed to abate. With his winnings from the cattle drive, he could easily help that dream come true for her.

''How about if I help you pay for it?''

Her eyes widened. ''You'd do that?''

''Consider it a gift.''

She smiled and sidled closer to him. ''I'll be happy to repay it any way I can.'' Then she leaned up to kiss him.

He gently held her off. ''Sorry, Marla, I'm already spoken for. You can repay me by becoming the best damn beautician west of the Mississippi.''

Tears gleamed in her big brown eyes. ''No one has ever given me anything before without expecting something in return.''

Matt thought of Calley and her unconditional love. "I know exactly how you feel."

"Radcliffe!" Tupper's voice boomed from behind them.

Matt turned to see the older man standing in the doorway of the study. He held a thick cigar in one hand and a glass of whiskey in the other.

"Get in here, son, before I decide to donate your check to some whiny charity." Then Tupper disappeared back into the room again.

Marla threw her arms around Matt's neck and hugged him tight. "Thank you, Matt. You don't know how much this means to me."

"I think I do," he whispered. Though he'd never been attracted to Marla, he knew her life hadn't been any easier than his own. She deserved a shot at happiness, too.

"Now go on," she said, shooing him toward the office. "Rufus is waiting."

But Matt knew more than Rufus Tupper was waiting for him. So was his future.

CHAPTER NINETEEN

"TAKE A LOAD OFF," Rufus said, standing at the wet bar in the corner of the study.

Matt sat down in a black leather wing chair opposite the big walnut desk. He couldn't help but compare this sprawling ranch house with the one he wanted to build. Rufus believed the bigger the better, but Matt didn't need a mansion. This place seemed cold to him. And empty.

Just like Rufus himself.

As Rufus uncorked a bottle of champagne, Matt's mind drifted back to the house he'd grown up in. Charles Mitchum had built his wife a huge Victorian home that had stuck out like a sore thumb on the stark Texas prairie. Even bigger than this place, the Mitchum's house had still seemed much cozier, friendlier. A place filled with love.

That's what Matt wanted. A home filled with light and laughter. And love. As his wife, Calley would bring all three to it. *His wife.* The thought made his whole body tighten. He didn't deserve a woman like her. But he was too damn selfish to give her up. And determined to work hard every day so he could give her anything her heart desired.

Rufus walked over to him and held out a flute of sparkling champagne. "I think this occasion deserves a toast."

Matt took the glass, wishing he could skip the formalities with Rufus. He'd much rather be out at the barbecue pit, celebrating with Calley and the crew.

"Do you want to make the toast or shall I?" Rufus asked, sitting down in a ponyskin chair behind his desk.

"The cattle drive was your idea," Matt replied.

Rufus grinned. "So it was. And one of the best ideas I've ever had, too. You should have seen the look on Hobbs's face today when he finally showed up and saw my herd was already in the corral."

"My crew put in a lot of hard work these last few weeks," Matt replied, just to remind Rufus he hadn't done it alone.

"To the best damn crew and the best damn trail boss in the country," Rufus said, lifting his glass in the air.

Matt took a sip of champagne. Despite the expensive label on the bottle, it tasted a little bitter on his tongue.

Rufus drained his glass, then licked his lips. "Not bad. Not as good as fine whiskey or a willing woman, but not half-bad."

Matt glanced at his watch. He couldn't wait until he was his own boss. When he could spend his time as he pleased, doing the work that he loved.

"Looks like you're in a hurry." Rufus rolled his chair up to the desk and opened a drawer. "So let's not waste any more time. I've got a personal check already made out in your name." He handed it across the desk. "Congratulations, Radcliffe. You've earned it."

Matt set down his glass, then reached for the check. His heart tripped in his chest—until he counted the number of zeros. Then he looked up at Tupper. "What the hell is this?"

"Your payment for a good month's work."

He tossed the check onto the desk. "This isn't what we agreed to."

Rufus rocked back in his chair, his glass cradled in his soft hands. "Five thousand dollars is a lot of money for a month's work."

"Our contract was for a hundred times that amount. You agreed to pay me five hundred thousand dollars if I won this cattle drive for you."

Reaching into the desk drawer once more, Rufus pulled out a sheaf of papers. "I think you'll see that our contract says differently."

Matt watched him turn over the top page, the champagne becoming sour in his stomach.

"The codicil on page 3, line 21," Rufus explained, then cleared his throat and began reading. "'The contractor—' that's me '—will pay the contractee—' that's you '—the amount agreed upon on page one, line five, in the event that the contractee crosses the finish line with the herd before the opposing team. In the event the contractee fails to do so, he will be paid a consolation fee in the amount of fifty thousand dollars from the contractor.'"

The smirk on Tupper's face was easier to read than a convoluted contract, and Matt didn't like what he saw one bit. "I won the damn race for you."

"But you didn't *personally* cross the finish line with the herd. According to Davis Gunn you toddled off to Jacksboro while the rest of the crew won the race for you."

Matt's eyes narrowed. "We had a medical emergency."

Rufus shrugged. "Hell, son, that's not my fault. Neither is the fact that you can't read a contract that spells out the exact terms in black and white. Guess your talents are limited to riding a horse and steering a bunch of cattle over the range."

"You son of a bitch," Matt breathed, his whole body coiled to leap across the desk and wrap his hands around Tupper's throat.

He smiled. "Don't take it so hard, Radcliffe. I'm willing to offer you a full-time job to make up for your loss. The Lazy R still needs a foreman. You belong in a saddle, Radcliffe. You're a natural there. And you sure as hell don't need half a million dollars to ride a horse."

Matt stood up, the blood pounding in his veins. It was gone. All of it. His dream. His ranch. The life he'd only dared to start imagining. "I don't need anything from you, Tupper." Then he picked up the check and tore it in half.

"No hard feelings?" Rufus called, laughing as Matt strode out of the study.

He walked past a gaping Marla and out the front door. Like a shooting star, his dream of owning a ranch had flared brightly for a few precious moments, then disappeared into the black night.

Now he just wanted to do the same.

"OKAY, CALLEY, spill it." Deb stood next to her at the barbecue pit, drinking out of a champagne bottle. "Something's happened, girl. You're positively glowing."

Calley had been surrounded by the crew as soon as they saw her. And she'd been incredibly touched by their concern for her. As amazing as it seemed, she'd found more than the love of her life on this cattle drive. She'd found something she hadn't had for too many years—good friends.

"All right," Calley replied with a smile, "but you have to promise not to spread it around. I want Matt to be here when we tell the rest of the crew."

Deb wobbled a little on her feet, obviously feeling the effects of the champagne. "You can trust me, Calley. I never, ever spill a secret. Well, except for that time Davis told me I was the best lover he ever had. But hell, what woman could keep a secret like that? And I only told some folks at my high school reunion in Laramie. The same folks who had voted me Most Likely to Be an Old Maid."

Calley reached out and hugged her friend. "I'm going to miss you, Deb."

"I'm not going anywhere," Deb countered.

"I am." She took a deep breath. "Matt asked me to marry him. We're going to buy a ranch here in Texas."

Deb stared at her, then a smile blossomed over her weathered face. "Hot damn. If that isn't the best news I've heard since Davis promised to quit wearing his boots to bed. I hope you're inviting us to the wedding."

Calley smiled. "I couldn't imagine it without you. In fact, Deb, I'm really hoping you'll agree to be my matron of honor."

"Well, hell." Deb took a deep, shuddering breath. "Now you're going to make me cry. Do you know how many years it's been since I wore a dress? Davis and I got married in blue jeans."

"We'll go shopping together," Calley promised, "and find something that's just right for you." She'd spent the last month just living one day at a time. Now she was looking forward to the future.

The sound of a slamming door made them both turn toward the ranch house.

"Isn't that your husband-to-be now?" Deb asked as they both watched Matt stalk off in the opposite direction.

"Matt!" Calley called out. But he didn't stop. Didn't even turn around.

"Probably can't hear you with those cowboys whooping and hollering," Deb said, motioning to the raucous crew behind them.

Maybe. But that didn't explain why he'd slammed the door. Or why he was walking away from them. "I think something is wrong."

"Rufus must have riled him again," Deb said, tipping up the bottle and taking a long swig. Then she rubbed her mouth across the back of her hand "That Tupper is worse than a splinter under a fingernail. He probably blasted Matt for not bringing the herd in even sooner."

Calley stared into the darkness. She couldn't see Matt anymore, but something inside her didn't feel right. She handed her champagne glass to Deb. "I'll be right back."

Following a worn path in the sparse grass, Calley searched for her cowboy. The howl of a lone coyote made gooseflesh prickle her skin. She wrapped her arms around her middle as she searched the shadows for a sign of the man she loved. Now far past the corral, she couldn't hear the sounds of the crew any longer and could just barely see the porch light glowing from the Lazy R ranch house.

Something scampered just ahead of her, causing

Calley to jump. Her heart pounded and she wondered why she was so skittish after spending so many nights on the open range. Less than an hour ago, she'd been on top of the world. Now, as she finally spotted Matt up ahead, something about the way he looked told her that world might come crashing down.

He didn't turn around as she approached, just stood leaning against an old mesquite tree, staring up at the night sky.

"Making a wish?" she asked softly, laying her hand on his shoulder. He didn't look at her and she could feel his muscles tense under her fingertips.

"There aren't any stars out tonight." His voice sounded flat and full of despair. "Besides, I don't believe in wishes anymore."

She moved in front of him, shaken by the hollowness she saw in his dark eyes. "Matt, what's wrong?"

"There isn't going to be any ranch, Calley. Tupper reneged on the deal."

"But how can he do that?"

His eyes finally met hers. "He can do it because he's a master at cheating people. And because I didn't take the time to decipher every word and nuance of that contract he had me sign."

"But that money rightfully belongs to you," she insisted, indignation for the man she loved flaring inside of her. "You earned every penny of it. We'll call a lawyer. We won't let Tupper swindle you out of money that is rightfully yours."

Matt shook his head. "He's too smart to leave any loopholes. I'm betting he had the best lawyers in the state look over that contract before I signed it. Hell, they probably drew it up for him."

Calley refused to let him give up. Somehow there

had to be a way to make it right. "I still don't understand. What was the loophole?"

His gaze flicked away from her. "It doesn't matter."

A cold premonition washed over her. "Tell me. If you don't, I'll find Rufus Tupper and ask him myself."

His eyes met hers once more. He reached out one hand and trailed his callused fingers over her smooth cheek. "According to the fine print in the contract, I was supposed to personally cross the finish line with the herd."

The impact of his words made her fall back a step. He hadn't been at the finish line because he'd taken her to the hospital in Jacksboro. "Me? You lost all that money because of me?"

He shook his head. "No. I only have myself to blame. I knew Tupper never played square with anyone. But I took the job anyway."

And Calley knew the reason why. Because he wanted a ranch of his own so very, very much. A place to call home. She stepped forward and wrapped her arms around him. "I'm sorry, Matt. I'm so sorry."

He just stood there for a moment, then placed his hands on her shoulders and held her at arm's length. "I already told you it's not your fault. I don't ever want you to think that."

"Let me talk to Tupper." Calley couldn't stand to see the desolation in his eyes. "I can tell him how the cattle drive was sabotaged and how you put a stop to it. How you worked both night and day to win his bet for him."

"No." His hands tightened on her shoulders. "I

don't want you anywhere near him. The man is like a leech. He sucks the integrity out of people and feeds on their weaknesses. I won't let him do that to you, too.''

"Then let's get out of here. Leave Rufus Tupper behind and forget he ever existed. He can keep his lousy money. We've got something more valuable anyway. Love. A future." A tremulous smile rose to her lips. "And I hope, someday, a family."

"Don't you understand?" Matt's hands dropped away from her. "I can't marry you now."

CHAPTER TWENTY

CALLEY STARED UP at him, the coolness in his voice chilling her to the bone. "That's ridiculous. Rufus Tupper might be able to take your ranch away, but he can't pull us apart. I love you, Matt. I want to spend the rest of my life with you."

"And I love you," he replied, still standing stiffly beside her. "And when I had half a million dollars dangling before me, I thought that was enough. But now I know I have to let you go."

She didn't like the finality in his tone. "I still don't understand."

"Cliff said it best—a man who can't take care of his family isn't much of a man."

"What does Cliff have to do with us?"

"He sold his integrity, Calley, because he didn't have health insurance for his family. Most cowboys don't. He and Katie didn't know they'd have twins someday. Or that a simple pregnancy could turn high risk. But we do know that you have a heart condition."

"And that's why you don't want to marry me? Because of my heart?" All her old insecurities came rushing back. Had that marriage proposal simply been a way to keep her fighting? A risk he wasn't willing to take now that his dream had died. Not only had he lost his ranch, but he was saddled with a chronically ill fiancée.

He closed his eyes. "I want to marry you so damn bad it's killing me to say I can't do it. You're the only person that matters to me in this whole world, Calley Graham. You always will be."

"Then prove it," she challenged. "Marry me."

"I can't."

"Can't or won't? The choice is up to you, Matt. If you don't love me enough, just say so. But don't make up excuses. For a man of your word, you certainly don't seem to have any qualms about breaking it."

He took a step closer to her, fire blazing in his eyes. "I'm breaking it to save your life! Before Tupper pulled his little trick, I believed I'd have enough money to buy my ranch, but more importantly, I'd have the assets necessary to take good care of you in case anything did happen."

"Nothing is going to happen to me."

"I pray that's true. But if I marry you, your father's health insurance won't cover you anymore. You're still listed as his dependent. That would change as soon as the preacher pronounced us husband and wife."

Her head spun and she fervently hoped this was all a hallucination. Some bizarre side effect of the heat stroke. She didn't want to face the reality. "So this is all about money?"

"No." He rubbed his hand over his unshaven jaw. "It's about love. I love you too much to take the risk of marrying you."

"And I love you too much to let you go." A lump rose in her throat, but she swallowed it back, determined not to resort to tears. "If it's the marriage that's a problem, then we'll just live together. As long as we're together, Matt, nothing else matters."

"I'm a cowboy," he replied, his face drawn. "I spend my life working on the open range, drifting from one job to the next. Even if I did find permanent work, most ranchers are conservative men. They aren't going to allow a hired hand to shack up with a woman on their place. And frankly, I want more than that. And so do you."

It was true. Calley wanted to do more than share a house and a bed with him. She wanted to share his name. Give him children. Take vows to love and cherish him before God and their family and friends.

Another dream that wouldn't come true.

"I'll leave for Trueblood in the morning," he said after a long moment. "So you can call your boss and tell him I'm on my way."

She swallowed hard, trying to focus on his words. "I didn't cross the finish line, either. You're under no obligation to go to Violet Mitchum's memorial service or anywhere else."

His eyes narrowed. "Despite what you may think of me now, Calley, I am a man who keeps his word. And I don't welch on a bet because of a technicality."

She nodded, realizing she'd lost her fiancé and won the consolation prize—a job at Finders Keepers. "Okay. We'll leave in the morning."

He shook his head. "You need to see your cardiologist. I can find the way to Finders Keepers on my own."

On his own. He couldn't have made his feelings any clearer. Maybe she'd been right the first time. Maybe Matt had simply had a change of heart. She couldn't argue with him anymore. Not when her own heart was threatening to shatter into tiny pieces. If he didn't want her, she wasn't about to force herself on him.

She nodded, then without another word, turned and walked away. Calley had chosen to live dangerously by falling in love with a cowboy.

And paid the price.

THE NEXT DAY, Matt sat in Dylan Garrett's office at Finders Keepers. He'd leased a pickup truck in Jacksboro, then spent most of the three-hundred-mile drive to Trueblood telling himself he'd done the right thing. Only he couldn't forget the expression on Calley's face when he'd told her their marriage was definitely off.

Dylan opened the folder on his desk. "I'll admit I'm a little surprised you got here so fast. Calley only called a few hours ago to tell me you were on your way."

Just hearing her name made him miss her all the more. "I'm anxious to put this all behind me."

Dylan nodded. "I'll do my best to arrange the memorial service within the week. Once I've worked out all the details, I'll have Calley contact you."

"I'd rather leave her out of this," Matt said bluntly. "I'll leave a number where you can reach me as soon as I check into a motel."

Matt could see the curiosity in the other man's eyes. He respected the fact that he didn't pry. In fact, his first impression of Dylan Garrett was favorable. He briefly wondered if Calley found him attractive. If she'd end up turning to Dylan or some other man on the rebound.

Just the thought of her in another man's arms made his gut tighten. Then he saw the framed photo of a slender blonde on top of the desk. Maybe Dylan didn't fall into the romantic rival category after all.

"Her name is Julie," Dylan said, following his gaze. "She's beautiful, isn't she?"

Matt nodded, unable to keep from comparing her with Calley. But he didn't want to tell Garrett that his woman didn't come close to matching Calley's sexy smile, mouthwatering figure and infectious vivacity.

Then Dylan turned to him. "I don't know what happened between you and Calley. Frankly, it's none of my business. But I do know how she sounded on the phone this morning. Almost as bad as you look this afternoon. And I've just got one piece of advice for you. Something I learned the hard way. Don't ever let go of the woman you love, because you might never get her back."

Matt swallowed, wondering if Dylan Garrett was psychic or just a good judge of human nature. He'd seen the man's service award plaques on the wall when he'd walked into the office. Garrett had obviously been a hell of a police officer to earn such acclaim. Matt wondered what had made him give it all up.

Maybe the woman in the picture?

Then he heard Tupper's voice echoing in his brain. *Guess your talents are limited to riding a horse and steering a bunch of cattle over the range.* He'd accepted Tupper's words as fact. But who said a man couldn't trade horses in midstream? Maybe he could find a way to keep Calley in his life after all.

He stood up abruptly. "Is there anything else you need from me today?"

Dylan looked up at him. If he was surprised by Matt's sudden mood change, he didn't show it. "No, I'll handle it from here. Just stick close to this area while I work out the arrangements for the memorial service. I should be in touch with you sometime in the next few days."

"I'm not going anywhere," Matt replied, moving toward the door.

And he meant it.

THREE DAYS LATER, Dylan Garrett walked into Sebastian Cooper's office and tried to ignore the rage that boiled up inside him every time he saw the man. It was hard to believe he used to call him his best friend. Even harder to believe that Dylan had let Sebastian steal Julie from him all those years ago. They had both paid a price, although Julie's had been much steeper than his.

Now Dylan was determined to make it up to her.

"Have you found my wife?" Sebastian asked, not wasting time on small talk. Their relationship had cooled considerably in the last couple of weeks—a change that Dylan didn't regret. Sebastian rarely returned his telephone calls now and had canceled more than one meeting.

"Nothing new yet," Dylan replied, taking a seat opposite the massive desk. "But Bill Simms is still working on it."

Sebastian snorted. "That guy isn't worth the cheap polyester suits he wears. He hasn't turned up any new leads about Julie. And Finders Keepers isn't exactly burning a trail to her, either."

The only thing that kept Dylan from punching Sebastian in the mouth was the knowledge that Julie and her son were safe in Cactus Creek. The longer Sebastian was kept in the dark, the better for all of them. "Actually, I'm not here to talk about Julie. Violet Mitchum's memorial service is scheduled for tomorrow afternoon at two o'clock."

"So?"

"I thought you might want to attend." Dylan wasn't sure why he was even extending the invitation. Violet hadn't been taken in by Sebastian's charm— in fact, the older woman had seemed wary of him, something Dylan had found unusual at the time. Still, Violet had given refuge to the two stranded friends after their car broke down, and Dylan felt it only fair to inform Sebastian of the service.

Sebastian shook his head. "I'm sorry, I don't have time to attend. Even though my wife is missing, I've still got a business to run. I've wasted too much time already chasing after her."

"Spoken like a man in love," Dylan said in a low voice.

Sebastian stared at him. "It's a little late for the jealousy routine, isn't it, Dylan? Julie chose *me*. She married me."

Before Dylan could reply, the intercom buzzed and the voice of Sebastian's secretary sounded over the line.

"Mr. Cooper, there's a Mr. Luke Silva here to see you."

Dylan glanced up quickly at Sebastian and saw the apprehension on his face. Luke Silva was the second in command of the local organized mob. The man in charge now that the ring leader, J. B. Crowe, was behind bars. Dylan hadn't had any luck connecting

Sebastian to Silva, but one look at Sebastian's expression told him all he needed to know.

Sebastian clicked the switch on the intercom, then leaned back in his chair. "Tell Mr. Silva this isn't a good time for me, Brenda. I'm in a—"

The office door slammed open and Luke Silva strode inside, followed closely by Sebastian's secretary.

Sebastian jumped out of his chair and rounded his desk, meeting him halfway. "I'm in a meeting."

"End it," Silva ordered, his eyes hidden behind a pair of dark sunglasses. He wore shiny urban cowboy clothes and his jet-black hair was slicked back into a ponytail.

"I'm sorry, Mr. Cooper," the secretary said, wringing her hands together. "I told Mr. Silva he needs to make an appointment."

Silva gave her an icy smile. "Why don't you take a break? Pick up one of those chocolate eclairs your boss likes so much from that bakery across the street."

"How do you know…" she began, until Sebastian interrupted her.

"Go ahead, Brenda," he said, nodding toward the door. "Take your afternoon break. I'll handle it from here."

She nodded, then walked out of the office.

Silva turned to Dylan. "I hope you don't mind cutting your meeting short. I have a matter of some urgency to discuss with Mr. Cooper."

Dylan glanced at the intercom, the tiny green light telling him Sebastian had forgotten to shut it off. He'd be able to hear every word outside the office.

"Not at all," Dylan said, rising to his feet. Then he nodded to Sebastian. "I'll be in touch."

But all of Sebastian's attention was focused on Silva. Dylan walked out of the office, closing the door behind him. The reception area was empty. Then he heard voices over the intercom. He sat down at Brenda's desk and pulled the unit closer.

"Are you crazy coming here?" Sebastian asked, sounding a little rattled.

"We need to talk."

"That man was Dylan Garrett," Sebastian continued, "the private detective I've hired to find my wife. He's a former cop with the Dallas PD. The last thing we need is him sniffing around the organization."

"Let's talk about your wife," Silva replied. "I think she's become a distraction for you. Some of the boys are concerned that you're not holding up your end of things."

"I don't give a damn about Julie anymore," Sebastian hissed. "But I suspect she's alive. And I'm almost certain she found out about my involvement with the organization. That's probably why she ran off in the first place."

"So eliminate her," Silva said evenly.

"That's my plan. But I need to find her first. She has something I need."

Dylan's blood ran cold. If he'd had any lingering doubts about Sebastian's feelings for Julie, they were crystal clear now.

"Something you need?" Silva chided. "Hell, Cooper, if you need a woman, just go to the nearest street corner."

"I wish it was that simple. Julie has possession of some…information. Only she doesn't know it."

A deadly silence followed, broken only by the crackle of static over the intercom.

"What kind of information?" Silva asked at last, his voice eerily calm.

"Information that could make you and J.B. cellmates if the cops ever got a hold of it," Sebastian replied. "So you might want to remember that the next time you get the urge to barge into my office. It's time for you to show me some respect in this organization. You never know, Luke—someday you may be taking orders from me."

Silva's laugh was low and chilling. "You think you can challenge me? I could make one phone call, Cooper, and you'd be dead within the hour. I detest men like you. Spineless worms who can't even control their own women. What makes you think you could ever control me?"

"I think you misunderstood me." Sebastian sounded worried. And well he should, Dylan thought, considering Silva's reputation. "I want us to work together."

Their voices grew lower and Dylan realized he'd be putting his own life at risk to stay here any longer. But one thing was clear.

Sebastian Cooper couldn't play his role as the worried husband much longer. He was finally beginning to unravel.

CHAPTER TWENTY-ONE

Liv Graham opened the front door, her smile fading when she saw who stood on the other side.

Matt removed his cowboy hat. "Hello, Mrs. Graham. I've come to see Calley."

"She's not here right now," Liv said, one hand still gripping the edge of the door.

"Do you expect her back soon?"

Calley's mother hesitated, her face hiding none of her anxiety.

"I did as you asked," Matt said softly. "I sent Calley back to you."

"Liv?" A male voice sounded behind her, and Bill Simms walked into view.

His eyes widened when he saw Matt, then he moved beside Liv, his stance that of a man protecting his territory. "Is there a problem?"

"He wants to see Calley," Liv blurted, "and I'm afraid he'll...upset her. She hasn't been the same since she's come home. What if—"

Bill laid a gentle hand on her shoulder. "She's a big girl, Liv. If she wants to see Radcliffe, all she has to do is track him down, just like she did before. Wouldn't you rather they meet here than have her run off again?"

Liv chewed her lower lip, obviously wrestling with Bill's calm logic. At last she opened the door wider.

"I suppose you may come in and wait for her, Mr. Radcliffe. But I can't promise she'll be here anytime soon."

Matt followed Liv and Bill inside the house. Photographs of Calley as a young girl dotted walls that held little else in the way of adornment. He slowed his step so he could look at each one, a visual montage of her life. First Calley as a baby, then a chubby toddler. In one photo, she sat on the shoulders of a man who must be Walt Graham, her blond hair in pigtails and a wide smile on her face. In another photograph, she hugged a dog. As he moved down the wall, Calley grew up before his eyes. Dressed as a pumpkin when she was about eight years old. Sitting astride a pony at about ten. Then brandishing a pair of pom-poms when she looked to be about fourteen.

The number of photographs thinned and he noticed one vital difference as he perused her late-teen years and early twenties. Calley didn't smile much anymore. Those had to be the years after her heart condition had been diagnosed. That in itself didn't give her much to smile about. Still, when Calley had shown up at the cattle drive, his first impression of her had been her sunny cheerfulness.

"Please have a seat, Mr. Radcliffe," Liv said, motioning toward the sofa. "May I get you something to drink? Coffee? Tea?"

"Please call me Matt." He set his cowboy hat on the glass-topped coffee table. "And some tea would be great."

She looked at Simms. "Bill?"

"Tea sounds good to me, too."

She nodded. "I've got some cookies in the freezer.

Chocolate chip." A smile fluttered over her lips. "They're Calley's favorite. I'll thaw some out for us and maybe a few extra to surprise her when she gets home." Then Liv turned to Matt, twisting her fingers together. "It could still be quite a while yet. I could have her call you if you'd just like to leave a number."

Matt knew in his gut that Calley would never get the message. "I don't mind waiting."

"All right," Liv replied, then walked out of the room, leaving the two men alone.

Matt turned immediately to Bill. "Why doesn't she want me to see Calley? Is something wrong?"

Bill sat down on the recliner with a heavy sigh. "Yes, but not with Calley."

Matt arched a brow. "Meaning?"

"Meaning this family is screwed up. I've only been around a few weeks, but it's pretty clear to me. Liv was a basket case when Calley was missing. Now that she is home, her mother treats her as if she were five years old instead of twenty-five. I've never seen anything like it."

"I noticed she's a little overprotective," Matt said, empathizing with the woman. He knew how it felt to rush Calley to the hospital, not knowing if she was going to live or die. Hell, he'd only known about Calley's heart condition for a couple of weeks and hadn't wanted to let her out of his sight. Liv Graham had lived with that uncertainty and fear every day for the last ten years.

Bill sighed. "Overprotective. That's an understatement if I ever heard one. Try smothering. Calley can't hardly take a breath without Liv hovering over her."

He leaned back in the chair. "That's probably the reason she's kept to her room ever since she came back home." Then he looked intuitively at Matt. "Or is there another reason?"

"That's between Calley and me," Matt replied, sitting up on the sofa. "And I'm starting to believe it might be better if we had our conversation in private."

Bill glanced toward the kitchen. "I think you're probably right."

"Do you know where Calley is right now?"

Bill hesitated. "Liv might never forgive me, but she's got to break this obsession she has with her daughter. Calley had a three o'clock appointment with Dr. Rice, her cardiologist. His office is in the medical building on Navarro Street—it's only about eight blocks west of here."

Matt glanced at his watch. It was already three-twenty. If he hurried he might still be able to catch her. He moved toward the door and almost ran into Liv, who had just emerged from the kitchen carrying a tray with iced tea and chocolate chip cookies.

"You're leaving?" Liv asked, her tone conveying both confusion and hope.

"Yes." He glanced at Bill, then back at Calley's mother. "Your daughter is an amazing woman, Mrs. Graham. You should be very proud of her."

Liv blinked. "Thank you. I am."

After Matt left, she walked into the living room, then frowned down at the coffee table. "He left his cowboy hat here. We can't let Calley see it."

"Sit down, Liv," Bill said gently. "We need to talk."

MATT WALKED through the glass door leading into Dr. Rice's office and straight to the reception desk. "Is Calley Graham still here?"

"Matt?"

He turned to see Calley seated in the small waiting area, a fashion magazine open on her lap. He drank in the sight of her, realizing the three days they'd been apart seemed more like three years. Her blond hair was pulled into a French braid, with silky wisps curled around her cheeks. She wore a simple denim dress and a pair of brown leather sandals. Her eyes looked even more blue than he remembered. She gazed up at him with an emotion he couldn't identify. Was it caution? Hope? Love?

"What are you doing here?" she asked at last.

"I had to find you." He walked over and sat in the chair next to hers. There was only one other patient in the waiting room, an elderly man who sat glued to the small portable television set in the corner. "Have you seen the doctor yet?"

She shook her head. "He's running behind, as usual." Then her brow furrowed. "How did you know I was here?"

"I stopped by your house."

The furrow deepened. "And my mother told you where to find me?"

He smiled at the disbelief in her voice. "No. Bill Simms did."

She licked her lips. "Matt, I could pretend that I'm not thrilled to see you here. But that would be a lie. My heart is pounding so hard it makes me glad a doctor is nearby. So I'd appreciate it if you'd tell me the reason you came here so I don't let my imagination run wild.'' Her voice lowered to a whisper. ''Or get my hopes up too high.''

He reached for her hand and gave it a gentle squeeze. ''I'm here because I can't live without you, Calley. And because I want to beg your forgiveness and ask for a second chance. You're not the only one who spent too much time out in the sun. It must have made me just plain crazy or I never would have let you go.''

''You didn't let me go,'' she said softly. ''You walked away. And how can I be sure you won't do it again?''

He took a deep breath. ''Because I decided to confront the problem facing us instead of running away from it. You've got a heart condition and I don't have the means to take proper care of you. So I did the next best thing. I just interviewed for a job that provides insurance coverage for my entire family, including coverage for preexisting conditions.''

Calley's expression grew even more guarded. ''What kind of job?''

''Working on an oil rig out in the Gulf for the Capitol Petroleum company. It's mine if I want it.''

''But you're a cowboy.''

His throat grew tight. ''I'm not anything without you.''

She let go of his hand. ''You belong on a horse, Matt. Not marooned on a steel platform in the middle of the Gulf. You'd hate it. And you'd grow to hate me for making you give up the life you love.''

''Now you're the one making excuses,'' he countered. ''I'm more than a cowboy. I'm a man in love with a woman. A woman who means the world to me. And you're the one who's crazy if you think I'd rather spend my time riding the range with a bunch of scruffy cattle. I love you, Calley Graham. And I want you to marry me.''

''Are you sure you don't want to hear the doctor's prognosis first?''

''He can't tell me anything I don't already know.'' He slid off his chair and knelt in front of her, not even caring what the receptionist would think. ''I refuse to waste another minute living in fear of what might happen. I'd rather spend that time loving you.''

She took a deep, shaky breath, still too wary to let herself believe him. ''You didn't feel that way three days ago, Matt.''

He smoothed his thumb over the back of her hand, seeking to allay her lingering doubts with each gentle stroke. ''Three days ago, I blamed Rufus Tupper and the world for cheating me out of the money I needed to buy a ranch of my own. But Tupper was right, I didn't deserve it.''

She stood up. ''That's not true!''

Matt rose to his feet. ''Tupper is a stupid man who made a stupid bet. I knew it going in, but I decided to trade my integrity for the chance to buy my own ranch. It was a bad deal. I lost my self-respect. And I lost you.''

''You didn't lose me,'' she replied, her defenses crumbling. ''You might have walked away, Matt, but I had every intention of coming after you. I just needed to come home for a few days to lick my wounds and see Dr. Rice. But I wasn't about to let you go so easily.''

''Even after the way I treated you?''

She smiled. ''You should know by now that I don't

let a cranky cowboy deter me. I was going to stay hot on your trail until you surrendered.''

Matt took a step closer to her, wrapping his hands around her waist. "I surrender."

"I always knew you were a smart man."

"Smart enough never to let you go again." He kissed her long and deep, then lifted his head just far enough to look into her beautiful blue eyes. "Will you marry me, Calley?"

The sound of a throat clearing made them both turn. A nurse stood in the hallway to the examining rooms with a folder in her hand and a scowl on her face. "The doctor will see you now, Miss Graham."

Calley nodded, then looked up at Matt. "Come with me? Just so you know what you're getting into."

"Absolutely." He reached for her hand. "From here on out, we're in this together."

CHAPTER TWENTY-TWO

CALLEY HELD her breath as Dr. Rice walked into the small examination room. She sat perched on the exam table, a layer of white tissue paper beneath her. Matt was seated nearby in a chair, giving her a reassuring smile. Her answer to his proposal could very well depend on the doctor's assessment of her condition. She wanted to spend her life with Matt, but she refused to anchor herself to him in marriage if it would cost him everything he held dear. Like his work. And his love of the land.

Somehow she'd find a way to be with him without becoming a burden.

"Hello, Calley." Dr. Rice approached her, his arms folded across his chest. "What brings you here today?"

Her fingers gripped the edge of the exam table, crinkling the tissue paper. "I thought it was about time for another checkup."

He frowned, then picked up her file. "Why?"

She blinked at his blunt question. "Because of my heart condition."

Calley wondered now if she should have made the appointment with her old cardiologist, Dr. Benning. Dr. Rice had only been her physician for the last six months, so she didn't know him all that well. Still, he did have her latest test results.

"We plan to marry soon," Matt interjected. "And we want to make sure it won't compromise Calley's health in any way."

The doctor closed the file. "I don't see any reason there would be a problem."

Calley glanced at Matt, growing a little frustrated by the doctor's obtuseness. "I quit taking my heart medication about three weeks ago. Then I suffered a case of heat stroke and the emergency room physician suggested I make an appointment with a cardiologist as soon as possible."

"What medication is that?" Dr. Rice asked, opening the folder again and flipping through all the papers.

"The Zenate," she replied, no longer able to hide her exasperation. "I've been taking it every day for the last six months. Just like you ordered."

The doctor stilled, his gaze locked on some typewritten notes. "Zenate isn't a heart medication." Then he looked at her and said softly, "Did your mother tell you I recommended she see a psychiatrist when I called your house with the test results?"

"No." A strange foreboding stirred in the pit of her stomach. "She just told me that the results weren't good, and that you were worried that I was doing too much and my heart might not be able to keep up. That's why you prescribed the Zenate. It was supposed to be a stronger medication."

"Hell." Dr. Rice tossed the thick file onto the counter, then rubbed one hand over his jaw. "Calley, there's nothing wrong with your heart or anything else. The day those results came in, I gave you a clean bill of health."

"Then why did you prescribe the medication?" Matt asked, a scowl on his handsome face.

"Zenate is a vitamin and mineral supplement," Dr. Rice replied. "And I only prescribed it to make Mrs. Graham happy. She insisted that Calley was seriously ill and nothing I said would sway her. That's when I suggested she get some therapy."

Calley stared at him. "You mean if I had answered the phone that day, you would have told me I was fine?"

He nodded. "I just found a memo buried in your file reminding me to call again and talk to you personally, because I suspected your mother might not be completely honest with you. But I must have gotten busy and forgot all about it. I'm sorry."

Calley didn't know what to say. Or how to feel. Anger at her mother was mixed with despair. She remembered all those times her mother would hover by the phone, waiting for the latest test results to come in. How long had Liv been lying to her about her condition? Had her mother wanted to control Calley so much that she'd let her live under a potential death sentence?

"I still don't understand," Matt said, rising to his feet and moving next to Calley. "Did her heart condition just resolve itself?"

"Calley had a condition called myocarditis, which causes an inflammation of the heart muscle and weakens it. Fortunately, a few patients are able to make a full recovery. It took a while, but Calley is one of the lucky ones."

Matt's thigh brushed against her leg. "What about the damage that was already done?"

"It was minimal. She was monitored for several

years to make certain the rest of the heart muscle could compensate. Calley's first cardiologist, Dr. Benning, gave her a series of tests and established just that, but Mrs. Graham wasn't satisfied and wanted a second opinion. So six months ago, she brought her daughter to me. I repeated the same tests, more to reassure Mrs. Graham than out of necessity.''

"Calley?" Matt asked softly, looking at her.

She swallowed, realizing she'd just been given her life back. It was an odd feeling, and one she wasn't entirely comfortable with yet. Part of her ached at the thought of all the time she'd lost and all the missed opportunities.

But if she'd lived her life differently, she might never have met Matt Radcliffe.

The doctor cleared his throat. "When I called your house with the test results, I just assumed your mother would relay the good news. I realize now the problem with your mother was even more serious than I thought."

"That's okay," she said, reaching for Matt's hand. "I think it may have all worked out for the best."

The doctor nodded, then moved toward the door.

"Oh, one more thing," Calley said, stalling his departure. "Is there anything in my medical history that would prevent me from having children?"

Dr. Rice looked from Calley to Matt, a slow smile spreading across his craggy features. "Not a thing. I'd just give you the same advice I'd give any woman—eat properly and put yourself in the care of an obstetrician."

"Did you hear that?" she asked after the doctor left them alone. "I can have your baby, Matt. More than one, if we want. Two, three, even ten."

He smiled "I think we're getting a little ahead of ourselves. You still haven't answered my question."

She hopped off the exam table. "What question?"

"Will you marry me?" Matt reached for her, encircling her waist. "It's the question I intend to keep asking until you say yes."

"Yes," she replied, wrapping her arms around his neck. "Yes. Yes. Yes."

He pulled her closer. "Now that's a word a man likes to hear."

THAT EVENING, Calley and Matt stood on the front porch of her house. The door opened before Calley had a chance to retrieve the key out of her purse.

"Where have you been?" Liv Graham demanded, her mouth thinning when she saw the man standing behind her daughter.

"Matt wanted to show me his hotel room," Calley replied defiantly, though she felt her cheeks warm. "It's right on the River Walk."

"May we come in, Mrs. Graham?" Matt asked.

Liv hesitated a moment, then nodded. "Of course, this is Calley's home."

They walked inside. Calley's legs still felt a little weak from the lazy afternoon she'd spent making love with Matt. He'd finally convinced her not to put off this meeting with her mother, claiming you couldn't move into the future until you dealt with the past.

"I've got some chocolate chip cookies," Liv began, moving toward the kitchen.

"We don't want cookies, Mom," Calley said abruptly. "I saw Dr. Rice today."

Liv froze. "And?"

"And I'm fine." Bitterness welled up in her throat

like bile, making it hard to speak. "Why didn't you ever tell me? I'm not sick anymore, Mom."

Liv paled. "We don't know that."

"Yes, we do," Calley exclaimed. "Dr. Rice made it perfectly clear. My heart is fine. I can do anything I want. Those pills I've been taking faithfully for the last six months are nothing more than vitamins. I'm probably the healthiest person on this block!"

Liv sank down on the sofa. "You don't understand."

"Then please explain it to me," Calley demanded. "Because at this moment, I'm not sure I ever want to see you again."

Matt stood by her side but didn't say a word, letting her fight her own battle. She wondered if he knew how much that meant to her. After nearly a decade of smothering protection, she was more than ready to stand on her own two feet. It was what she'd tried to tell him at the Lazy R, when his sole concern had been his lack of money and health insurance.

She didn't need a man to take care of her. Just one who loved her.

Liv sank down on the sofa, clutching a throw pillow on her lap. "The first time you got sick, the doctor told us there was nothing we could have done to prevent it from happening. But I knew that wasn't true. I was your mother. I was supposed to protect you. But I'd just accepted an invitation for a photo exhibit in New York City. I was too preoccupied with my work to keep a good eye on you. Somehow, some way, you got sick."

The tremor in Liv's voice made a crack in the hard shell of Calley's anger. "How can you say that? People get sick all the time. It wasn't your fault."

Her mother looked up at her. "One day you were

perfectly healthy, and the next day the doctor is talking about a heart transplant. That doesn't just happen. There has to be a reason.''

For the first time, Calley wondered if her mother had suffered more these last ten years than she herself had. Liv had lost her marriage and her friends and her work in her fierce determination to care for her daughter. But Calley wasn't ready to let go of her anger. ''That still doesn't explain why you kept the truth from me. I deserved to know.''

''Because I didn't believe it was the truth.'' Liv tipped up her chin. ''I'm still not certain. You read all the time about all the mistakes doctors make. What if those test results are wrong? What if something happens to you when I'm not paying attention?''

Calley sat down on the sofa beside her mother. ''I'm twenty-five years old. You can't protect me forever. And what's more important, I don't want you to. I want to live my own life. Make my own mistakes. And you're not responsible for either one.''

Liv gripped her hand so tightly it hurt. ''But I love you.''

''I hope so,'' Calley said gently, ignoring the pain. ''Because if you really love me, Mom, you'll let me go.''

Liv looked up at Matt. ''Go where?''

''Matt asked me to marry him,'' Calley explained. ''We haven't decided yet where we're going to live or what we're going to do. We just know we want to be together.''

Matt nodded. ''And we'd like your blessing, Mrs. Graham.''

''But even if you're not ready to give it, I'm ready

to live again.'' Calley took a deep breath. ''With or without you in my life.''

Liv's lower lip trembled. ''That doesn't leave me much of a choice. What if—''

''No more what-ifs,'' Calley interjected. ''I want you to see someone, Mom. A therapist or a counselor.''

''Bill wants me to see one, too.''

''I think it will help both of us move on with our lives.'' Calley gave her mother's hand a gentle squeeze. ''This house was more like a prison to me than a home. But I realize now it's been a prison for you, too. It's time for both of us to be set free.''

''Can I think about it?'' Liv asked. ''Bill wanted to take me out for supper this evening. I told him no, because I knew you'd be here...''

''I won't be here,'' Calley informed her. ''I'm going with Matt.''

Liv gave a jerky nod. ''Then maybe I'll accept Bill's invitation. I...like him.''

''I think that's a very good idea.'' Calley smiled. ''And I like him, too.'' Then she gave her mother a fierce hug.

Liv hugged her back, her body shaking with silent sobs. Calley looked up at Matt and silently mouthed her thanks. He'd been right about confronting her mother. It was the first step toward healing the pain of the past.

Now she just needed to convince him to take his own advice.

''I THINK WE SHOULD have stayed in bed,'' Matt said the next morning as he drove a rented pickup truck into Pinto. "I feel strange about going to a memorial service for a woman I haven't seen in twenty years."

Calley smiled at him. "Who was it that said we have to deal with the past before we can face the future?"

"Obviously some idiot who was too besotted to think straight."

"Hey, watch it," Calley admonished cheerfully, "I happen to be in love with that besotted idiot."

He narrowed his eyes. "That comment is going to cost you a kiss."

"I'm not sure it's proper to kiss at a memorial service."

He sighed. "Another good reason to skip it."

"Are you afraid?"

The question made Matt flinch. As usual, Calley was both perceptive and straightforward. "The last time I saw Violet I was twelve years old and the west wing of her house had just burned down. We didn't part on the best of terms."

"So now you're wondering why she remembered you in her will?"

Matt glanced at her. "More like *how* she remembered me in her will. I can't help but wonder if this is some form of retaliation. She believed I was responsible for the fire."

"You really think she's reaching back through the grave to seek vengeance?"

He shrugged. "I know it sounds stupid, but I can't figure out any other reason why I'm here."

She held out her hand. "Just remember, cowboy, you're not here alone."

Reaching over to take it, Matt wondered how he'd gotten so damn lucky. The answer was simple: Violet

Mitchum. If she hadn't named him in her will, Calley never would have tracked him down. So despite his reluctance, he'd show his appreciation by paying his respects to the woman who had once been like a mother to him.

Calley leaned back against the headrest. "I called Deb this morning while you were in the shower and told her the wedding was back on."

"I still don't believe you'll ever get that woman into a bridesmaid dress."

"You won't believe what she told me about Rufus Tupper, either."

Matt glanced at her, noting the mischievous gleam in her eyes. "What?"

"Rufus went on a three-day drinking binge to celebrate his win. Only he must have gloated one too many times, because his buddy Lester Hobbs shot him in the leg."

"I know I shouldn't say so, but it couldn't have happened to a nicer guy," Matt said, grinning.

"Wait, it gets even better. When Hobbs got charged with assault, he copped a plea by turning over evidence of tax fraud on Rufus."

"So nobody wins," Matt said, turning into the long gravel drive that led to the large Victorian house he had once called home.

"Nobody except us." Calley squeezed his hand, then looked out the front window. "Is this it?"

He nodded, looking up at the familiar light-blue house with white trim and white latticework on the peaks. Except for a new extension on the wraparound porch, it looked exactly as it had before the fire. "Charles built this place for Violet in the fifties. He wanted her to feel like a queen."

A fleet of vehicles was already parked in the circular driveway. Matt positioned the pickup behind a black Lexus, then switched off the engine.

"Ready?" Calley asked.

He turned to her. "Not until I get that kiss."

She obliged, cradling his jaw with her hand as her mouth melded against his own. His body tightened and he wondered if his desire for her would ever be sated. At last she lifted her head and smiled at him.

He smiled back. "Now I'm ready for anything."

CHAPTER TWENTY-THREE

DYLAN GARRETT waited in the library while the people gathering for Violet's memorial service slowly wandered inside. It was Violet's favorite room. Fully stocked bookcases with her beloved romance novels lined the walls and a grand piano graced one corner.

When he spotted Matt Radcliffe entering with Calley Graham at his side, Dylan grabbed the bulky sealed envelope he'd brought with him and walked over to them.

"Glad you could make it," Dylan said, holding out his hand.

Matt shook it, his grip firm, but his gaze wandering around the room. "It's been a long time since I've stood in this house. It brings back a lot of memories."

"Violet wanted you to have this," Dylan said, handing him the envelope.

"What is it?" Matt asked.

"The ring she bequeathed to you, along with a letter."

Calley looked up at Matt. "Do you want to open it now?"

"Later." Matt took the package. "After the service."

Dylan nodded, then walked to the front of the room. Everyone had arrived and was now finding seats among the three rows of folding chairs set up in the center of the library. Sara Pierce and her fiancé, Justin Dale, sat in the front. Next to them were Jillian Salvini Peterson, her husband, Mark, and their son, Drew. Stella Richards, owner of the Blue Moon Café, sat in the second row next to John Carpenter and his daughters. Matt and Calley took their seats in the third row along with Mary Barrett and Stuart Randolph.

He cleared his throat. "Good afternoon. We're gathered here to celebrate the life of a truly remarkable woman, Violet Mitchum. She was the beloved wife of the late Charles Mitchum, and a friend, confidante and advisor to countless others. That's why it's no surprise that she left the bulk of her estate to start a foundation to help people in need. Each of her beneficiaries will receive a generous monetary bequest, along with a sentimental gift. Because she specifically requested that the eight beneficiaries named in her will be here today, in lieu of a eulogy, I think each of us should share how Violet came into our lives." He smiled. "And since it was my idea, I'll go first."

Scanning the faces in front of him, he noted that Matt Radcliffe was the only one who looked slightly uncomfortable with his suggestion. The man obviously didn't want to be here, which only made Dylan more impressed with Calley Graham's persuasive skills.

"I met Violet four years ago when a friend and I went on a fishing trip and our car broke down just outside of Pinto," Dylan began. "The first house we saw looked like it belonged in London instead of the Texas prairie." He smiled. "And there was Violet waving to us from the front porch. When we explained our predicament, she generously offered to let us stay with her until the repairs were done.''

He took a deep breath. ''My mother had recently passed away, and I was still feeling guilty for not being there to say goodbye. When Violet told me how much she loved horses, I found myself telling her how my mother had taught me to ride. And how much I had loved her.''

Dylan saw Sara wipe a tear from her eye, shaking his own vow to hold his emotions in check. ''Violet and I went riding that day, although she'd been too frail to ride for years. I held her in front of me while we rode across the prairie.'' He swallowed hard. ''It was as if I were given a second chance to tell my mother thank-you and goodbye. Violet's bequest to me was that horse. But she gave me so much more.''

Dylan sat down abruptly, his throat too tight to continue.

Jillian stood up and gave them all a watery smile as she pointed to the piano. ''That's my gift from Violet, and it's being moved to my new home next week. She not only encouraged my music, but my dream to study interior design.'' Jillian turned to gaze at her husband and son. ''She taught me that dreams really can come true.''

Stuart Randolph, the grandson of the man who lent Charles the equipment to dig his first oil well, received the first dollar Charles Mitchum ever made. He spoke of Violet's compassion for those less fortunate.

John Carpenter choked up as he related the many hours he and Violet had spent in the stable, where he tended her precious horses. A devout man, he treasured the family bible she'd left him.

Stella Richards fingered the beautiful sapphire necklace Violet had left her and told of the meals she'd sent from the Blue Moon Café when Violet was too ill to cook for herself. And how she'd been repaid ten times over by Violet's steadfast friendship and confidence in her.

Mary Barrett, who was well into her eighties, cherished the writing desk Violet had left her and told how much she missed her friend and the long letters they used to share.

Then Sara Pierce stood up, not bothering to check the tears streaming down her cheeks. "Violet literally saved my life. She gave me advice when I needed it most. But more important, she made me understand that real love transcends fear and guilt and betrayal. That to have faith in someone else, you must have faith in yourself first."

Sara held up a packet of yellowed envelopes tied with a faded pink ribbon. "Violet left me the love letters she and her husband Charles sent to one another throughout their courtship and marriage. And in them I've found proof that true love really can survive anything."

When Sara sat down, Justin's arm went around her shoulders, pulling her close. Silence descended over the room and for several long moments the only sound was the loud ticking of the grandmother clock on the wall. Then the last beneficiary slowly rose to his feet.

Matt Radcliffe.

MATT'S GAZE scanned the faces turned expectantly toward him. These were people Violet had loved. And their fond memories of her had helped him remember all the good times he'd shared with her. Times that definitely overshadowed their last painful day together.

He looked down at Calley, who gave him an encouraging smile. Then he opened up his heart. "I grew up in this house, the son of the Mitchums' housekeeper. But neither Violet nor Charles ever treated me like a servant. Especially Violet. She took me to the circus when I was five. Held me on her lap when the clowns frightened me. And gave me a pony of my own for my seventh birthday."

With each word Matt spoke, a little of the bitterness faded away. "When I was ten, the class bully gave me a black eye and a bloody nose. As soon as she saw me, Violet picked up the phone and called her husband, who was over one hundred miles away overseeing the drilling of a new well. She told him there was an emergency and he had to come straight home."

He smiled at the memory. "You should have seen Charles Mitchum's face when he found out the *emergency* was teaching me how to fight. But he did it anyway. Violet had rummaged through the dusty attic and found an old pair of boxing gloves for me to wear. I guess I'll never know if it was the boxing lessons or a secret telephone call from Violet, but Johnny Ray never bothered me again.

"Violet gave me so many gifts when I was growing up that I could never remember them all. But I do remember the most important one. She taught me to respect myself and to be proud of who I am." He glanced at Calley, moved by the tears he saw gleaming in her beautiful blue eyes. "And she taught me something else, too. Real love never ends."

But Matt knew he couldn't stop there. It was time he lived up to Violet's faith in him. Time he took responsibility for his part in their estrangement. "I wish I could say I never let Violet down, but that wouldn't be true. When I was twelve years old, I accidentally started a fire that destroyed part of the house she adored."

He hesitated a moment, letting that information sink in. Several of the beneficiaries glanced at each other and he heard a few furtive whispers. Sara Pierce stared up at Matt, her brow furrowed.

"It's too late to make it up to her now," he continued. "But I know that Violet found a way to forgive me. Because she just didn't have room in her generous heart for anger or bitterness." Then he sat down and reached for Calley's hand, drawing on her strength and love.

Dylan rose to make one last announcement. "According to Violet's wishes, we're to spend the afternoon riding her prized horses, then proceed to Stella's Blue Moon Café for some of the best barbecue in Texas."

As the rest of the guests slowly filed out of the room, Calley wrapped her arms around Matt and squeezed him tight. "Have I mentioned lately that I'm crazy in love with you?"

Matt glanced at his watch. "Not for at least an hour."

"Well, then let me make up for lost time." She leaned over to kiss him, then pulled back, her gaze fixed over his shoulder.

Matt turned to see Sara Pierce standing there with Justin Dale. John Carpenter stood close behind them.

"I'm sorry to interrupt," she said, "but John and

I talked about it and we think there's something you should know.''

John placed an old Bible on the chair in front of him. "This belonged to the Mitchums.''

"I know," Matt replied, recognizing it. "Violet always kept it on a mantel in the drawing room, behind a glass case.''

Sara held out a tattered envelope. "Read this first. Then look at the page that's bookmarked in the Bible.''

Matt took the envelope, but before he could ask any more questions, they turned and walked away.

Calley watched them leave. "Well, that was certainly mysterious.''

They were alone in the library, though Matt could still hear the chatter of voices in the foyer. He turned the envelope around and looked at the postmark. "This is dated one month after the fire. It's from Violet to Charles.''

"Are you going to read it?''

He nodded, and Calley placed her hand on his knee. He pulled the letter out of the envelope and unfolded it, recognizing Violet's neat, flowing script.

Matt read aloud.

"My darling Charles,

Yes, I forgive you. These past weeks have taught me that I love you too much to live without you. I've tried to spend all your money here in Dallas, but ended up buying both of us new wardrobes. Maybe that's a sign that it's time for us to start over.

I miss my home. And my horses. But most of all, I miss my husband. I won't pretend that the betrayal didn't hurt. But what hurt me even more was the fact that you kept it from me for so long. I believe you when you tell me you were too drunk to remember the incident yourself...but we both know it didn't end there."

Matt looked up from the letter as icy prickles of apprehension rose over the back of his neck. "I don't think I want to read any more."

"Shall I?" Calley asked softly, holding out her hand.

He hesitated, then gave her the letter.

"'But we both know it didn't end there,'" Calley continued, her quiet voice calming the storm brewing inside of him. "'And as long as we're both finally being honest with each other, I should tell you that some part of me always knew.'"

"Knew what?" he asked.

She glanced up at him, then turned her gaze back to the letter and took a deep breath. "'I think that's why Matt so easily captured my heart. Deep down inside I knew he was your son.'"

He closed his eyes. "No."

Calley read silently for a few moments, then set the letter in her lap. "I think it's true, Matt. According to the rest of the letter, one of the servants blamed you for setting the fire and wanted to call the police. Your mother came to Charles and begged him not to let it happen."

"I think I can guess the rest," he said flatly. "Violet overheard her tell Charles I was his son."

Calley nodded. "The letter intimates that they were together only once, and that Charles was very drunk at the time."

"So that's why Violet ordered me out of her sight." Matt rubbed one hand over his jaw. "Not only had I tried to burn down her house, she'd just discovered I was her husband's bastard son."

"I think you should listen to the last part of Violet's letter," Calley said, then began reading again.

"While I can freely forgive you, Charles, because I've never doubted your love for me, I don't think I can ever forgive myself. In my pain, I lashed out at Matthew—the only innocent in all of this. Innocent of even starting the fire, according to that electrician's report. Every time I remember the hurt I saw in his big brown eyes, it makes me cry.

Matthew is the son of your body and the son of my heart. We have to find him, Charles. I'm coming home to you today so we can begin the search. And begin our lives again.

Yours forever,
Violet."

Matt picked up the Bible, then reverently opened the worn black leather cover. One by one, he turned the stiff pages until he came to one with the Mitchum family tree.

Calley trailed her finger down the page, then stopped near the bottom. "Matthew Todd Radcliffe, son of Charles Mitchum and Rita Radcliffe."

"So it's true," he murmured, the shock finally beginning to fade. "And it explains so damn much. Todd Radcliffe wasn't my real father. He must have known the truth when he married my mother. Maybe it's one of the reasons he left us."

"She never said anything to you?"

He shook his head. "Or to Charles, obviously, until the day of the fire. No wonder she was so adamant about us leaving in the dead of night."

"Are you all right?" Calley whispered.

He nodded. "Just a little numb."

Calley picked up the bulky envelope Dylan Garrett had given to him before the service. "Violet wrote a letter to you, too. Do you want me to read it?"

He took a deep breath, then nodded again, not trusting himself to speak.

She undid the clasp on the manila envelope, then reached inside and pulled out a single sheet of lavender stationery.

"'My dearest Matthew,'" Calley began, holding the letter in front of her.

"If you're reading this, it means I've found you at last. Charles and I searched for you all those years ago, but when we learned your mother had changed her name and was trying to start a new life, we thought it best to respect her wishes.

I've always wondered if we made the right decision. Just as I've wondered if you were ever able to forgive me.

You're not responsible for that fire, Matt. Or for the cruel words I spoke that day. My heart was broken for an entirely different reason and I'm ashamed to say I took it out on you.

Please know that I love you and that Charles always loved you, too. If you look in the Mitchum family Bible, you may be better able to understand. But what's most important to me is for you to know one thing. I would have given anything on this earth to be your mother. And no son could have made me prouder. I'm wearing the ring you gave me all those years ago. And I've already given instructions that I am to be buried with it. My life will end before long, but my love for you never will.''

Calley's voice broke, and she took a deep, shuddering breath before she continued. ''As Charles Mitchum's son, you belong here, Matt. So I'm leaving you this house and horse ranch. And something else that is most precious to me. I pray you have a happy, loving life, my son. And please know that I'll be looking out for you. Love always, Violet.'''

Calley placed her arm around his shoulders and held him until he finally got his emotions under control.

''This is turning out to be one hell of a day,'' he said at last, wiping his face.

She reached into the envelope and pulled out the deed. ''I believe you're now the owner of one of the most prized horse ranches in Texas. And the most *unusual* house.''

He gave a choked laugh. ''I'm still trying to believe it myself.''

''Well, once you get used to the idea, you might want to think about advertising for a hired hand. Because Dylan Garrett offered me a job at Finders Keepers. The best part is that I can work out of an office in Pinto.''

''You mean you'd rather chase down missing people than missing cows?''

She laughed through her tears. ''Absolutely.''

Matt grew thoughtful. He could help Marla pursue her beauty school dream. And maybe he could help someone else as well. This was a day for redemption. And forgiveness. "What if I offered a job to Cliff? I think Pinto is the perfect place to raise a family."

She leaned over to kiss him. "And I think that's the best idea you've ever had."

"The second best," he said, reaching into the envelope. He pulled out a white velvet box and reverently opened it. "The best idea I ever had was asking you to marry me."

Calley's breath caught in her throat when she saw the diamond-and-sapphire ring nestled inside.

"This was Violet's wedding ring," Matt said solemnly, taking it out of the box and holding it in his palm.

"It's beautiful," Calley breathed, watching the gems on the band sparkle in the sunlight streaming through the window.

"Violet gave me something that was the most precious to her. Now I want to give it to the person who is the most precious to me." He reached for her left hand, then slid the ring onto her fourth finger. "Let's make it official, Calley Graham. I want the world to know you're all mine. Now and forever."

Calley smiled up at him. This time she saw more than love shining in his eyes.

She saw the future.

TRUEBLOOD, TEXAS
continues next month with
THE SHERIFF GETS HIS LADY
by Dani Sinclair

Sheriff Noah Beaufort didn't know what to make of the mysterious Skylar Diamond. He couldn't believe she was really a stalker, though her presence in tiny Bitterwater was pretty suspicious. And Skylar didn't dare tell him the truth. That she was the mother of his adopted daughter...

CHAPTER ONE

"NOAH!" ALMA SAID. "You have to do something."

Too late to hide, Noah thought ruefully, and strode over to Alma. "Afternoon, Alma. What do I have to do something about? I'm not even on duty right now."

"Ha! You're the county sheriff, you're always on duty. Besides, you know young Terry's still wet behind the ears. This woman would chew him into little pieces."

The idea of anyone chewing his six-foot-three-inch, two hundred twenty pounds of muscled deputy into little pieces made Noah smile.

"What woman, Alma?"

"The one over in my café. She's been hanging around Darwin Crossing for two days now. She doesn't belong here." Alma's seamed face creased even further.

"Where does she belong, Alma?"

The older woman sniffed. "City woman. Now I ask you, what business could she possibly have here in Darwin Crossing? As the sheriff, you should talk to her. Find out what she's up to."

He tried to keep amusement out of his voice as he tipped back the brim of his Stetson and tilted his head.

"You mean you haven't pumped her for information already?" There was no better source of information in town than Alma Underwood. The woman lived for gossip.

"Hmph. Not that one. You can't pump her with a twelve-gauge. She's real cool-like. Cuts you dead with a look. Good lookin' broad, I'll give her that, but only if you like the snooty type. She comes into my place and just sits there watching."

"Sitting's not illegal, Alma. Neither is watching. And you do own the only café in town."

The older woman scowled. "She doesn't come there to eat. She orders perfectly good food and then sits there playing with it while she looks out the window or scribbles away on this pad she carries."

Alma took her food seriously. Noah kept his grin hidden and glanced over at his pickup to be sure it wasn't blocking anyone.

"I guess city women are picky eaters, but I'm afraid that isn't illegal either."

Alma set her jaw and eyed him from beneath thick round glasses. "Okay, I didn't want to say this right out, Noah, but if you're gonna take that attitude, now I will. She seems to be watchin' your Lauren."

"What?"

Amusement vanished at the mention of his daughter's name. Noah came away from the fender of her SUV. Tension took a two-fisted grip on the base of his stomach.

"Thought that might get your attention."

From the day Beth and he had adopted Lauren, he'd always secretly feared that one day Lauren's birth mother would come and try to take their little girl away.

"Are you sure about this, Alma?"

"'Course I'm sure."

Who would be watching his daughter?

"A woman," he said almost to himself. The adoption had been perfectly legal and nearly twenty years ago. Still, Beth's death had strengthened the fear. What if Lauren's biological parents learned that Beth was dead? What if they decided they'd made a terrible mistake? He'd never understood how anyone could give up a precious baby like Lauren in the first place. His fear had not abated after Beth's funeral. It even played a small role in his moving out here in the middle of nowhere after he found himself a widower. Strangers were always noticed here in Darwin Crossing.

"'Course she's a woman, didn't I say as much?"

"Who is she?" he demanded.

"That's what you need to find out."

SILHOUETTE *Romance*™

Escape to a place where a kiss is still a kiss...
Feel the breathless connection...
Fall in love as though it were
the very first time...
Experience the power of love!

Come to where favorite authors——such as
Diana Palmer, Stella Bagwell,
Marie Ferrarella and many more——
deliver heart-warming romance and genuine
emotion, time after time after time....

Silhouette Romance——
stories straight from the heart!

Silhouette®
Where love comes alive™

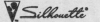

Where love comes alive™

From first love to forever, these love stories are for today's woman with traditional values.

A highly passionate, emotionally powerful and always provocative read.

SPECIAL EDITION™

Emotional, compelling stories that capture the intensity of living, loving and creating a family in today's world.

Silhouette

INTIMATE MOMENTS™

A roller-coaster read that delivers romantic thrills in a world of suspense, adventure and more.

Visit Silhouette at www.eHarlequin.com